ANGELA BRITNELL

◆

TAKE A
CHANCE
ON US

Complete and Unabridged

LINFORD
Leicester

First published in Great Britain in 2017

First Linford Edition
published 2019

A catalogue record for this book is available
from the British Library.

ISBN 978–1–4448–4032–2

Published by
F. A. Thorpe (Publishing)
Anstey, Leicestershire

Set by Words & Graphics Ltd.
Anstey, Leicestershire
Printed and bound in Great Britain by
T. J. International Ltd., Padstow, Cornwall

This book is printed on acid-free paper

Another Madcap Scheme

'I've got an amazing idea, Becky. Listen to this.'

The shine in her cousin Susannah's blue eyes surely meant trouble — exactly as it did when they were children and Susannah dreamed up another madcap scheme.

In the twenty years since they last saw each other the only huge change was the American accent that had taken Rebecca by surprise yesterday.

They'd drifted apart after her aunt and uncle moved their family to Nashville but already it felt as though they'd never been parted.

'I need to get out of Nashville for a good long while. Assuming there aren't any major problems with the computer network when the new hotel opens in early March I'll turn things over to my assistant and take a leave of absence.

1

My boss totally gets that I can't hang around and watch Tom marry someone else.'

Susannah's heartbreak over the recent break-up from her long time boyfriend was palpable and Rebecca ached for her cousin.

'I've gotten lazy recently so I thought of hiking the Cornish coastal path. Dad always talks about it in a wistful sort of way and if nothing else it should help clear my head.'

'You're welcome to the spare bedroom for as long as you want.'

'Thanks but no thanks.' Susannah grinned. 'My brilliant proposal is that we do a house swap for a couple of months. What do you think?'

'A house swap? Are you crazy?'

'Come off it, Becky, you're as stuck as me. I'm guessing if you chuck in your dreary building society job you'll have plenty to live on for a while. You've already admitted your social life is a big fat zero.'

'Chuck in my job? I'm quite content.'

'Liar.'

Rebecca's cheeks burned.

'You'd love my house in East Nashville. It was built in 1910 but it's been rehabbed and is totally cool now. It's what they call a cottage but you'd say it's a bungalow. There are tons of amazing restaurants and off-the-wall shops nearby.'

'I couldn't. I . . . '

'Why not? There's nothing keeping you here,' Susannah persisted. 'Are you still scribbling stories?'

Rebecca answered with a small shrug.

'I'll take that as a yes. When we were kids you always wanted to write a book, so why not have a go?'

'Don't be ridiculous,' Rebecca scoffed. 'You used to say you'd win an Olympic gold medal in ice dancing one day but childish dreams are precisely that. A few silly short stories written when I'm bored don't amount to anything.'

'You've changed.' Susannah stared her down. 'I know you've been through a heck of a lot but I hate that it's taken away all your sparkle and zest for life. I can't get my head around why you even stayed in this house.'

She didn't attempt to defend the choice she'd made to remain after the fire. Logically she should have sold up and made a fresh start but it had seemed impossible at the time and Rebecca simply let it drift.

Memories of Harry and her parents were all around in her mother's favourite cat ornaments and Harry's football trophies. Friends and co-workers lauded her for her strength but she sometimes wondered if that was a good thing.

'Drop it. Please.' Something about her quiet plea got through Susannah's brash confidence because she fell silent. 'I'll think about it and give you an answer tomorrow.'

'Fair enough.' Susannah jumped up. 'I'll go and put the kettle on.'

Rebecca remembered the other occasions when she'd succumbed to her cousin's bright ideas. One day they tested their superpowers by jumping off the garage roof which landed her in the hospital with a broken leg. Another disaster shattered her mother's prized crystal vase and led to her pocket money being docked for six months.

Her thirty-three-year-old self learned more than a few lessons the hard way.

*　*　*

'Daddy, did you see me?' Harper flung her hot arms around Zac's neck. 'Can I go home with Ava? Her mom's going to do our nails and she's making meatloaf. Please Daddy, please.'

'Hang on a minute, kiddo.' His beautiful daughter still bounced with energy after her demanding ballet class. Years ago Zac never pictured being a single father but every day with Harper was a gift, no matter how hard.

Even after nearly ten years he still struggled to understand Louisa's reasons for leaving them both when their daughter was two weeks shy of her first birthday.

'I can't do this any longer,' she'd said. 'I'm a terrible wife and mother. I warned you I would be but you wouldn't listen. I'm leaving before I do any more damage.'

'Daddy, are you listening to me?' Harper yelled.

'Of course I am.' Zac touched her hot red cheek. 'Quiet down, sweetheart. You were awesome today and Ms Ellen told me she'd picked you to do a solo in the recital.' Harper's beaming smile warmed him.

'Before we talk to Ava's mom tell me what homework you've got tonight.'

The sunny face disappeared and Harper muttered something under her breath.

'What was that?'

'I've got a spelling test in the morning.'

Zac wasn't sure which of them dreaded the weekly spelling test most. He hated being the bad guy and grilling her over and over until she melted into despondent tears.

'Ava's mom is real good at spelling.

She'll help us study.'

He resented the wave of relief surging through him before remembering his mother's recent telling off.

'You're a wonderful father,' she'd said, 'but that doesn't mean being a saint. Accept help when it's offered, Zac, dear. It won't hurt Harper one bit.'

'I suppose, if she doesn't mind, it's OK with me.' As soon as the words left his mouth Zac received another Harper-sized hug and his daughter raced off to see her friend.

Ten minutes later he stood outside the studio with a bag of ballet clothes and the prospect of three free hours. He'd suppressed a pang of sadness when his daughter happily grabbed Robin Wingate's hand, chattering about what colour she wanted her nails painted and whether Ava's mother could plait her hair.

Zac did his level best but he struggled with some of the things a nearly eleven-year-old girl needed and the next few years promised to be tough.

Zac's phone buzzed.

'Hey, sis, how's it going?'

'I've got two things for you,' Nikki said. 'A job and a date.'

'I'm interested in the first but not the second.' Were all sisters loving, persistent and eternally annoying?

Being the youngest of five might have something to do with it but Nikki Quinn didn't know the meaning of the word no. She'd been spoiled by their parents who assumed their family of four boys was complete until nine months after their silver wedding anniversary when Nikki arrived.

'But Jessica Taylor is an absolute sweetheart. You two would make a great . . . '

'No, Nikki. I don't care how perfect she is, I've got my hands full. Between Harper and work I don't have the time or energy to date.' Zac felt her pout over the phone. 'Tell me about the job.'

'I will but I'm not giving up.'

'The job.'

'Your least favourite, I'm afraid, but

I've no-one else free. It's helping an old lady in Fairview clear out her attic.'

Zac suppressed a groan. His irrepressible sister started Handy Helpers while she was still in high school and the business immediately took off. They specialised in the small, offbeat jobs other contractors weren't interested in taking on. Most of her crew were women because she'd discovered a gap in the market with customers who weren't happy opening their house to a strange man.

'I'll do it.' He didn't work for Nikki full time but slotted in helping her out between gigs as a session musician in the many recording studios on Music Row.

'You're a star.'

'Yeah, I know. Anyway, what're you up to?' Changing the subject was essential before Nikki returned to singing the praises of the amazing Jessica.

'I know what you're doing and I'll let you get away with it for now, because you're sweet enough to fill in when I'm desperate. If you're genuinely interested

I'm going to hear the Time Jumpers at 3rd and Lindsley tonight with a few friends. Hey, why don't you come along? Mom and Dad would love to take care of Harper.'

An evening spent listening to the famed, eclectic group of musicians versus homework, bath time and watching 'The Princess Diaries' for the 1000th time. For a second Zac wavered but his conscience kicked back in.

'Thanks but not tonight.'

'You always say no. When you're fifty and Harper's off living her own life what's yours going to be like? Pretty darn dull and empty if you ask me . . .'

'I wasn't asking.' He cut her off. 'I need to go. Ballet clothes don't wash themselves. Send me the job details and I'll be there.'

'I know you will.' A few seconds dead silence hung in the air. 'Louisa knew you'd always be there, too, didn't she?'

'Bye, Nikki.' Zac gently hung up and shoved the phone back in his jeans pocket.

His sister was right on several different counts but he'd no intention of admitting the fact any time soon.

Unexpected Offer

'But you're not a woman!' Rebecca's vehement accusation made the man standing outside her door smile. She fought to hold on to her glare in the face of his smile. It blossomed all the way to his warm chocolate brown eyes and before he opened his mouth Rebecca knew a deep, smooth drawl would trickle out. After a couple of weeks in Nashville she should be immune . . .

'Is that a problem?'

'Maybe.'

'Let me take a wild guess. You expected Nikki or one of her handy-women.'

'I did receive that impression when we spoke on the phone. Who are you, anyway, if it's not a bold question?'

'Zac Quinn, I'm Nikki's brother.' He stuck out his hand and waited, tilting his head to one side and glancing at her from under improbably long dark lashes. Rebecca grasped his hand and a spark zinged all the way down to her toes. 'I work for her part time when I'm not . . . '

'Do let me guess. Trying to become the next chart-topping country music singer? Every waiter and taxi driver I meet seems to believe they're the next Blake Shelton — whoever he is.' She tripped out the scathing putdown and Zac's eyes hardened. 'I'm sorry. That was incredibly . . . '

'Rude? Judgmental?'

Rebecca's cheeks burned.

'How about we give this another try? Good afternoon, Ms Tregaskas. I work for Handy Helpers and I'm here to take a look at your plumbing. Here's my identification.'

She felt obliged to take the card he held out.

'Thank you, Mr Quinn.' She couldn't unbend now and retain any shred of dignity. 'Please come in.'

Zac's mischievous smile galled her.

'Kitchen or bathroom?'

'Kitchen or bathroom what?'

'Um, where the leak is?'

Now he'd think her stupid as well as rude.

'Under the kitchen sink.'

'I'm sure you get asked this all the time but you're not from around here, are you?'

Rebecca gritted her teeth.

'No.' When she'd agreed to her cousin's suggestion that they house-swap for three months she'd never expected to be such a source of interest.

'Just no? Sorry. I'll quit the friendly conversation, fix your leak and get out from under your feet.'

His gentleness got to her and Rebecca bit back tears.

★　★　★

Why couldn't he learn to keep his mouth shut? A simple plumbing job, that had been Nikki's only request

14

when she rang him before lunch in a panic. Upsetting the customer wasn't part of his assigned task.

'Are you OK?' he ventured.

'Absolutely fine.'

Yeah, and I'm the Queen of Sheba, he thought.

'Glad to hear it.' Zac held up his tool bag. 'Kitchen?'

Silently he followed her across the living room, unable to avoid noticing her neat, curvy figure in well-fitting dark jeans and a soft blue hip-skimming T-shirt.

'I turned off the water and cleaned up the best I could.'

Of course the job wasn't straightforward. If Zac hadn't been aware of Rebecca watching from a vantage point across the kitchen his language would have slipped at several points but he restrained himself to a couple of mild oaths, the sort his mother couldn't object to. After an hour and a lot of huffing and puffing he finally finished.

'There you are. All done.' He

gathered up his tools. 'Nikki will send the bill.' Zac ran a hand through his messed-up hair.

'You missed a bit.' Rebecca playfully pushed away a stray strand and the soft brush of her fingers over his face startled Zac. 'I'm sorry. I shouldn't . . .'

'No apology needed. I'm the one with the misbehaving hair that won't do anything it's told,' he quipped. 'Unfortunately my daughter inherited it. Every morning we have a battle to get a comb through the tangles.'

'How many children do you have?'

'Only Harper, who's ten going on about fifteen.' His rueful response dragged a smile from Rebecca.

Her eyes narrowed and it was simple to follow her train of thought over why Harper's mother wasn't doing her hair. Should he let her ask or casually explain? This was a plumbing job not a date.

'I'd better be off.'

'Of course. We don't want to keep your other customers waiting.'

'I'm done with S bends for the day.' Zac laughed. 'It's tutus and pink tights next.'

Rebecca's eyebrows shot up.

'Not on me.'

'Thank goodness. You don't strike me as a pink tights sort of man.' She wrinkled her nose. 'You might get away with white or black but definitely not pink.'

Her witty response stirred another rush of unwanted interest in Zac.

'I can't be too fussy. Finding anything in my size is tricky.' Her sparkling gaze swept over him doing strange things to his insides.

'I can only imagine.'

A tease of perfume drifted his way, clean and sharp with an undertone of spicy heat. Zac cleared his throat and focused on getting away unscathed.

'Harper does ballet on Monday and Thursday. Tuesday is Girl Scouts. Wednesday's swimming and Saturday is soccer during the season.'

'She's a busy girl.'

'She loves it all.' Zac tried not to sound defensive. Being a single father seemed to give people permission to ladle out unsolicited advice. 'I don't want her missing out simply because . . . Sorry. I'm rambling.' For several lingering seconds Rebecca's gaze held steady and he couldn't look away. Very deliberately he broke the connection. 'If you have any more problems give Nikki a call.'

'I will and thank you for rescuing me. Or rather my pipes.'

'You're welcome.' He made a beeline for the front door and resisted the urge to say anything else.

★　★　★

After staring at the blank computer screen all afternoon Rebecca gave up. So far the change of scenery hadn't done much good and there'd been no miracle turn-around in her life. Yesterday she had considered cutting her losses and going back home but the thought of Susannah's scathing reaction stopped her calling the airline and changing her ticket.

In four weeks she hadn't written a single word, at least not one worth saving, and her plan to be more social hadn't materialised, either. At least her old job had forced her to talk to customers and the other staff whereas here she could go for days without speaking to anyone.

Rebecca grabbed the newspaper and sat at the kitchen table while she waited for the kettle to boil. She struggled to concentrate on an article about increasing traffic problems in Nashville but couldn't get Zac Quinn out of her head.

Good-looking men didn't usually wriggle under her skin but Zac's innate kindness when he realised she didn't want to talk and the loving way he spoke about his daughter — those things got to her.

Goodness knows what he'd thought when she'd switched from appallingly rude to borderline flirtatious in a matter of minutes. He wasn't to know that both were a million miles from her normal steady behaviour.

She had only rung Handy Helpers because they were at the top of the list Susannah left behind in case she had any problems with the house.

'Nikki's really cool and I don't know about you but sometimes tradesmen in my home make me uneasy,' she had said. 'The company does everything from plumbing to electrical work, carpentry and house sitting. Pretty much anything. And if she can't help you Nikki will know who can.'

Rebecca glanced out of the window at the clear blue sky and flung the newspaper to the floor. Maybe a long walk around the neighbourhood would shake her out of this lethargy.

She tracked down her shoes in the bedroom and as she struggled with the laces a loud knock on the door took her by surprise. She squinted through the peephole at a young woman with an eerily familiar smile.

'Hi, I'm Nikki Quinn. I was on my way home and thought I'd stop by to make sure everything's good now.'

'Oh, right.' Rebecca opened the door to this female version of Zac. 'Come in.'

'Were you on your way out?'

'Uh, yes, but only for a walk. It can wait.'

'Would you mind if I tagged along?'

Before she could come up with an excuse Nikki's unwavering gaze fixed on Rebecca and she could have sworn the girl saw right through her reticence. Were the Quinn siblings both mind readers?

'I'd enjoy your company.' Rebecca forced out a smile.

'If you don't have anything planned, I'm starved because I skipped lunch. We could get an early dinner at the Pharmacy. I bet it's one of your favourite spots.'

'I haven't tried it yet.' Eating out on her own rated pretty low on her wish list.

'Wow, that's hard to believe. Didn't

Susannah give you the low down on everything around here? This used to be a rundown part of Nashville but these days it's thriving. It's got a quirky unique vibe that you won't find in the Gulch. That's all fancy condos and people to match. At least I think so.' She rattled on, barely stopping to draw breath. 'I share a similar house to this with a couple of girlfriends a couple of blocks from here. Before we go, are you sure my big brother fixed your leak OK?'

'Yes, thank you. He was very . . . efficient.' Two circles of heat lit up her cheeks and she hoped Nikki didn't notice.

'Good. He doesn't work for me full time but I can always rely on Zac.'

'I'll lock up and we can go.' Rebecca didn't plan on discussing Zac Quinn with anyone, least of all his inquisitive sister.

Knocked For Six

Grease trickled down Rebecca's chin with a dribble of egg yolk but she didn't care. She hadn't realised a burger could be so good until she took her first bite of the Farm Burger Nikki insisted she tried.

With its unusual toppings of salty country ham, applewood smoked bacon, a farm-fresh egg and maple-laced mustard she'd never tasted anything like it before.

'Now you've started to eat, don't you dare put it down,' Nikki warned. 'Burger virgins always do that and the whole thing falls apart.'

'Burger virgins? I've never heard of such a thing.'

'Trust me. I went to London once and your excuses for a hamburger are something I've been trying to forget ever since.' She manufactured a visible shudder. 'But I've got to give y'all credit — you sure know how to do fish and chips. I fell in love with roast beef and Yorkshire puddings, too.'

'I'm glad something passed your strict food criteria.' Rebecca's sly aside didn't go unnoticed and the younger woman blushed.

'Sorry, I . . . '

'I'm joking.'

'You got me there.' Nikki flashed a broad grin. 'Susannah caught me out a couple of times, too. You're a lot like her. How're you related again?'

'Our mothers were sisters.'

'Were?'

After five years it still hurt to talk about her parents in the past tense.

'Mine passed away a while ago.'

'Sorry. I didn't mean to pry.'

'It's OK. Susannah's parents lived here for a long time but they recently moved to Florida when Uncle Pete retired.' Rebecca took another bite of her burger, partly because it was so good but also to grab a breathing space in the conversation.

She had already found herself telling Nikki far more than she'd intended when they set off on their walk. Still, she shouldn't complain. Through Nikki's eyes she'd had a taste of the vibrant neighbourhood with its wide range of small shops, cafés and restaurants.

'What made you start your business?' She'd turn the tables and ask a few questions herself.

'My dad's a plumber and I always loved helping him out. It kind of grew from there.' Nikki's warm laugh was the duplicate of her brother's. 'I was the only girl in my grade who preferred to re-plumb a toilet rather than put on a perky outfit and wave pom-poms around as a cheerleader. My poor mom despaired of me.' She rolled her eyes. 'Still does, sometimes.'

'Are you the only girl in your family?'

'Yep, four noisy boys and then they got me.' She finished off her beer. 'It's completely their own fault for celebrating their twenty-fifth anniversary a little too . . . exuberantly.'

'Gracious!'

'Not a word they'd choose to describe me,' Nikki teased. 'What about you?'

'In what way?'

'Have you got any siblings?'

The burger in her mouth turned to sawdust.

'No.'

'When they're nagging me and being annoyingly protective I think it'd be fun to be an only child but deep down I totally love my brothers.'

I loved mine, too, Rebecca thought.

'It's time I was going.'

Nikki's face lit up.

'I've got a brilliant idea. What are you doing the rest of the evening?' Before Rebecca could make up a suitably vague answer her companion blithely carried on. 'I'm meeting a few friends at one of the best live music venues in Nashville — 3rd and Lindsley. There's an awesome group playing tonight and it'll be a neat introduction to the music scene here for you. Come with me.'

She started to protest but Zac's sister was a veritable steamroller.

'We'll go to my place and do ourselves up a bit. My housemates Rae-Lynn and Suzy B are coming, too. We can call a cab and easily make it in time because the show doesn't start until eight.'

Rebecca needed to develop a backbone. She'd ended up in Nashville because she couldn't say no to Susannah and now she was being dragged to some awful show because of being so weak-willed. It served her right.

★   ★   ★

So much for separation anxiety. You're the one with that, idiot, Zac thought. Harper had snatched her overnight bag from his hand and raced inside the Wingates' house without even a good-night kiss.

'Are you sure . . . '

'Yes. I told you Adam's in New York

27

on business so we're going to have a girly night. Rosie's here, too, and the three of them do great together,' Robin insisted. 'Homework first and then dinner before we get to the fun part.'

'They've got school . . . '

'I know that, Zac.' A smile played over her face. 'They won't stay up late and I promise not to paint their nails bright scarlet or dye their hair purple.'

'I never said you would,' he protested.

'Ah, but you thought it.' Robin gave him a gentle shove. 'Off with you. Enjoy a night out for once.'

Were all women in a conspiracy against him? If he didn't know better he'd suspect Nikki of being behind Robin's spontaneous offer to keep Harper for a sleepover, but as far as he knew they'd never met.

'I'll have my phone with me but it might be noisy . . . '

'I'll text if there's a problem.' She held up a warning finger. 'Do NOT call me unless you've got an emergency. You do trust me to take care of Harper, don't you?'

'Of course. I wouldn't leave her else.' Zac trotted out the lie. 'Goodnight and thanks again.'

He trudged over to his truck and got in before snapping his seat belt in place. Zac noticed Robin watching from the front door and gave a hearty wave before driving off and heading towards downtown.

Half an hour later he'd snagged one of the last parking spots left along Third Avenue South and made his way inside the packed club. He checked his phone and fought back a grin as he read the message.

Harper's fine. Put the phone away and don't pull it out again for at least thirty minutes. Robin.

He scanned the crowd and spotted Nikki across the room in the middle of a group of women. It was impossible to miss her wild halo of curls, always tied back for work but let loose tonight.

Zac wended his way over and tapped

her on the shoulder.

'Zac! I don't believe it!' She flung her arms around his neck. 'Has the world come to an end and no-one told me?'

'You're not as funny as you think,' he grouched. 'Harper's having a sleepover with her friend Ava.'

'Seriously?'

Her incredulity jolted Zac. Was the idea really so surprising? When it sunk in that Louisa wasn't coming back he'd devoted himself to raising his daughter but maybe he was harming Harper by neglecting to have a life of his own, too.

'Hey, I'm only teasing, big brother. I'm thrilled.' She grabbed his arm. 'You know Rae-Lynn and Suzy B.' Nikki pulled him towards the two smiling women and waved her hand at the other woman sitting with her back to him. 'And I'm pretty sure you know this lady.'

'Ms Tregaskas, fancy seeing you here.' Zac stumbled over his words as she turned around. A rush of heat warmed her face and he took perverse pleasure from realising he wasn't the only one knocked for a loop.

'Nikki didn't say you were coming.' The sharp look she flashed his sister was one he'd used himself many times. Zac couldn't blame her for being suspicious.

'She didn't know. I turned down her offer yesterday but things . . . changed, and I was able to get away.'

'Get some drinks in, Zac, before the show starts,' Nikki ordered.

He couldn't put his finger on why Rebecca looked so different tonight. She wasn't plastered in make-up but her eyes appeared more luminous while her lips held a hint of something deep pink and glossy. Thin black straps held up a silky camisole and exposed creamy skin he knew would be soft and warm to the touch.

'Zac, drinks?' Nikki's strident voice startled him out of his reverie.

Three women stared at him with obvious amusement but Rebecca's expression was totally different. He suspected she'd been hit by the same bolt of recognition and equally knocked for six.

He was in deep trouble.

Bittersweet Memories

Rebecca struggled to pull her attention away from Zac but tonight he looked even better than she remembered. A black open-neck shirt rolled up at the elbows and tucked into snug-fitting black jeans, scuffed black cowboy boots and that warm smile on his lean, tanned face.

'What can I get you to drink, Ms Tregaskas?'

'Rebecca.'

'I haven't heard of that one. Is it a new cocktail?' His teasing drawl deepened her blush and she thanked heaven for the dim lighting.

'I meant you can call me Rebecca.'

Zac playfully slapped the side of his head.

'Boy, I sure am dumb tonight.'

'Get in a round of frozen margaritas, Zac, and hurry it up,' Nikki berated her brother.

'Yes, ma'am. Gotta do what my baby sister says or I'll be in trouble.' He grinned.

She nodded and sank back in the chair as he disappeared towards the bar.

'Is there something going on no-one's told me about?' Nikki plopped down next to her.

'What are you talking about?' Innocent pretence was Rebecca's only hope.

'Uh, maybe the meaningful glances zapping between you and my dear brother?' She prodded Rebecca's arm. 'Don't bother denying it. Y'all saw it, didn't you?' Nikki canvassed her friends and high-fived them when both agreed wholeheartedly.

'He's a . . . nice man. I'm sure Zac's friendly to everyone.'

'Nice? Friendly? Oh, come on. He hasn't looked at any women that way since the appalling Louisa ran out on him and my sweet niece nearly a decade ago.'

Rebecca would love to know more about the 'appalling Louisa' but must put a stop to this dangerous speculation.

'Look, Nikki, please drop it. I'm only

here for a couple of months and not interested in any sort of relationship.'

'Why not? Do you have a boyfriend back home?'

'No, and I'm not planning to interview your brother for the position.'

'What position? Did I miss something?' Zac reappeared with a tray of drinks.

'Resident plumber.' Rebecca snapped into preservation mode. 'I'm talking about how you rescued me this afternoon.'

Her breath caught in her throat and she crossed her fingers, praying the other women would play along.

'I'll come riding in on my white charger any time you need saving.'

Under the light-hearted response she sensed something deeper but chose to misunderstand.

'Your truck is probably more practical.'

He nodded.

'Yep, it sure is. Nashville has more gas stations than stables, plus the hot weather will really kick in soon, and horses don't have air conditioning.'

Rebecca laughed; she simply couldn't help it and neither could he. Surrounded by a bubble of mutual good humour nothing else existed for a few magical seconds.

'The show's about to start. For heaven's sake pass those drinks round, Zac, before we all die of thirst,' Nikki ordered. 'We'll all shift so you can sit next to Rebecca.'

She threw him an apologetic smile but he gave a good-natured shrug and followed orders. It wasn't hard to appreciate a man who could take a joke and patently loved his sister.

★   ★   ★

'Was Nikki hounding you?' Zac lowered himself into the chair and whispered in Rebecca's ear. When he accidentally brushed his mouth over her silky hair it released a waft of perfume to torture his overwrought senses.

'Hounding? No. Nosy? Maybe.'

'Sorry.'

'It's not your fault.' She touched his bare forearm and Zac instinctively wrapped his fingers around her slender hand. 'Tell me about the group who are going to play.'

The raspy plea knocked a little sense back into him and he loosened his hold.

'The Time Jumpers are pretty special.' As the musicians took their places on the stage he pointed out each of the ten members to Rebecca. 'They're all amazing country musicians in their own right with a host of awards between them. They came together to have fun and do something different outside their usual work.'

'Recapturing what drew them to music in the first place?'

Zac nodded.

'And it worked. They started playing a smaller club called the Station Inn on a Monday night because it's the quietest night of the week and eventually outgrew that and moved here.'

'I don't know much about country music.'

'You don't need to. They play everything from traditional country to Western swing, bluegrass and a touch of jazz. Bound to be something you'll like.'

Her blue eyes latched on to him and Zac forgot how to breathe. Luckily the band struck up the first bars of an old favourite of his, 'Sugar Moon', and he forced himself to shift a few inches to his left away from temptation.

'Here we go.'

As always the music drew him in. When Louisa left it had been his saviour, giving him a place to express the emotions he dared not release anywhere else.

He watched Rebecca from the corner of his eye, tapping her foot and humming along. The group went on to Willie Nelson's 'Sweet Memories' and the lyrics of loss and regret twisted his heart into knots.

He caught Rebecca's quickly suppressed sob and slipped his arm around her shoulders. It didn't seem wrong or out of place, only the most natural thing. Later he might question himself but not now.

Zac assumed she'd move away when the song ended but her head stayed resting on his shoulder, close enough she must be aware of his racing heartbeat. Nikki gave him a searching look but when he didn't react she glanced away again.

The set ended and the band broke up to take a short break. Some headed backstage and others went to the bar but one man leaped off the stage and made his way towards them.

'Hey, Quinn, what're you doin'? Seeing if we've still got it?'

Zac sprang to his feet and pumped the older man's hand.

'Yeah, well, someone's got to.'

'Zac, aren't you going to introduce us?' Nikki interrupted. 'You didn't tell us you actually know one of the Time Jumpers.'

'Know us? He's played with most of us one time or another, ma'am.'

Zac caught Rebecca's surprise and guessed he'd have some explaining to do.

'This is Andy Reiss. You won't find a better electric guitar picker anywhere in Nashville. He's a California boy originally but we try not to hold it against him.'

'We love this guy.' He slapped him around the shoulder. 'Wish you'd spend more time in the studio, Quinn.'

'Life, Andy. Too much goin' on.'

Getting into the tricky subject of why he'd allowed music to take a back seat in his life wouldn't happen tonight.

Zac quickly introduced everyone, passing Rebecca off as Nikki's English friend.

'I'd better get back. We'll have a few beers one night and catch up.'

'Sure.' It probably wouldn't happen but the thought was there.

They settled back down but Zac scooted his chair back slightly this time and concentrated on the second half of the show.

'I need a favour, big brother.' Nikki sidled up to him as they all stood up ready to leave.

'What is it this time?'

'Don't be snarky. I'm going to stay here awhile with Rae-Lynn and Suzy B. We want to kick our heels up a bit but Rebecca would rather go home and I wondered if you'd give her a ride?'

Be a bit more subtle, sis, Zac thought. Throwing us at each other won't work.

'I'm happy to get a taxi. It's fine,' Rebecca intervened. 'Please don't trouble yourself, Zac.'

The sensible side of his brain pushed him to accept the escape clause she'd offered.

But he couldn't forget the soft warmth of her skin under his fingers and the gut-wrenching recognition when she reached into his soul with her steady blue gaze.

'It's no trouble. I'm headed that direction anyway. But it's up to you.'

The flash of gratitude crossing her face pleased and bothered him equally.

'I mean that,' he murmured.

'If you're sure it's OK I won't be all stuffy and British about accepting.' Rebecca's tiny smile allayed his concerns. 'Have a good time, girls, and thanks for bringing me along tonight. It's been an eye-opener.'

Zac rested his hand in the hollow of her back as they made their way through the crowd and didn't hurry to move it away when they got outside.

'My truck's a little ways down the road.' They strolled along together in comfortable silence. 'Here we are.'

'Who's babysitting your daughter tonight?'

He yanked out his phone.

'She's having a sleepover with her best friend Ava. I can't believe I forgot to check for messages.' Rebecca's brow furrowed. 'It's OK. Not your fault. It's me thinkin' about myself . . . '

'For once?'

'Don't you start.'

'What did I say wrong?'

'Nothing, honey.' Zac caressed the

curve of her cheek. 'I get a lot of grief from my family about Harper. They think I should dump her on other people and get out more. Have a life.' He stared into Rebecca's eyes, seeing only sympathy in their dark blue depths. 'She is my life,' he whispered.

'Check your phone.'

Her quiet suggestion left him with the uneasy feeling the conversation wasn't over.

A Touch More Than Friendly

Ask him in for coffee. Don't ask him in for coffee. Question him about his music. Don't question him about anything. Rebecca's brain did somersaults as they neared her temporary home.

'I used to be a full-time musician.' Zac broke the silence. 'Mainly session work in recording studios although I've done a lot of live performances, too.'

'Used to be?'

'The lifestyle doesn't gel with being a single parent because the hours tend to be long and unpredictable.' The explanation sounded like one he'd given many times before. 'And, yeah, I miss it but . . . Harper deserves better than a part-time father.'

'I agree.'

'You do?' He tossed her a surprised glance. 'You're the only one who does.'

Rebecca smiled.

'You're not being fair on your family and friends.' His expression turned to stone. 'I'm sure they'd say the same but it doesn't mean you're doing the two of you any favours by centring your whole life around her either.'

An uncomfortable silence filled the vehicle and Zac stopped the truck outside Susannah's house. In the yellow glow from the street light his eyes narrowed on her.

'You don't have children, right?' She shook her head. 'Have you been through a rough divorce?' Zac ploughed on. 'Bad enough you needed to hire a private investigator to track down your ex before you got free of them?'

'No,' Rebecca stammered.

'Plus you've known me all of two days and have never met my daughter.'

'True, but . . . '

'But nothing.' He cut her off. 'I'd appreciate you keeping out of my private life.'

'I'll be happy to! I obviously misunderstood back at the club.' Rebecca bristled.

'I could've sworn you were being friendly — in fact some women would judge your behaviour as a touch more than friendly.' She yanked off her seat belt. 'I won't trouble you again. Thanks for the ride.' Rebecca fumbled for her keys in the bottom of her handbag.

'I'm sorry, I didn't . . . '

'Goodnight.' Flinging open the car door she took off running.

Zac watched her go safely inside and exhaled a deep sigh. The prospect of facing his empty house didn't help his unsettled mood. Zac cracked a half-smile at the irony. He had never admitted this to anyone but there had been a lot of nights when he longed for a few hours on his own.

In the old days he'd have channelled his emotions into music but it had been years since he had the time or energy to write anything. Hearing Andy Reiss and the others tonight, ten successful musicians making a living doing what they loved, stirred up a longing he'd largely managed to suppress. The occasional studio gig fitted in around the rest of his life didn't scratch the itch the same way.

Zac rubbed his eyes and started up the truck. He sure as heck wouldn't sleep tonight so maybe he'd try pouring out tonight's seesaw of emotions the old way and see what happened.

One last glance at Rebecca's house. One final thought of trying to put things right with her. The downstairs lights turned off and a few seconds later one popped on upstairs. No more chances tonight.

She'd handed a song title to him on a plate.

* * *

Curled up in bed with her laptop Rebecca's fingers couldn't keep up with the torrent of words tumbling out of her head. Zac's rejection stung but also gave her the germ of a story.

A Touch More Than Friendly.
Chapter One.

47

Near dawn she couldn't keep her eyes open and the screen started to blur. She saved her work and set the computer on the floor before snuggling down under the soft duvet. Zac's deep brown eyes fixed angrily on her were the last thing she remembered before drifting off.

★　★　★

The trickle of light filtering in through a gap in the curtains made Rebecca groan. She groped around on the bed-side table for her clock and struggled to sit up and focus on the numbers. After several attempts she admitted she'd been right the first time and it really was 11 o'clock. No wonder her stomach growled.

'I'd appreciate you keeping out of my private life,' he'd said.

'No problem, Mister Quinn!' Rebecca's shouted promise reverberated around the bedroom. She tossed back the covers and swung her legs around.

Maybe he'd done her a favour, because for too long she'd drifted along simply getting through each day. Her parents and Harry would be the first to applaud her new-found desire to change. If Susannah hadn't pushed she'd still be trundling through her normal unexciting routine.

After a quick shower she threw on some clothes and hurried downstairs to find something to eat. The fridge wasn't exactly bare but nothing lurking there set her taste buds alight. Yesterday Nikki had pointed out a place serving great tacos when they were out walking and Rebecca struggled to remember the restaurant's name.

Cornwall didn't exactly abound with Mexican food but she hadn't come to Nashville to replicate her everyday life. What precisely she'd come here for was a good question but sitting in the house on her own wouldn't provide the answer.

It didn't take long to track down Mas Tacos Por Favor online. Supposedly it was the place to get cheap authentic tacos and another benefit was its proximity to the Pharmacy, so she knew in which direction to head.

Five minutes later she hesitated outside Mas Tacos Por Favor. The place was no five-star restaurant but a rundown cement block building with bars at the small windows. If Nikki hadn't talked it up so much she'd never have considered venturing in.

'Rebecca! Are you searching for a hangover cure, too?' Rae-Lynn's raucous laugh startled her as the bubbly redhead appeared at her elbow.

'Oh, hello. Um, no . . . I'm just looking for lunch.'

'Please tell me that you and the super hot Zac . . . '

'No!' She'd squash that bizarre idea before it could take root. 'He gave me a ride home. That's it.'

Rae-Lynn's smile drooped.

'Drat. We really thought you two were hitting it off.'

'Who is 'we'?'

'Nikki and Suzy B, of course.' The other girl wasn't in the least perturbed about admitting their prurient interest. 'We couldn't believe Zac turned up in the first place. He's practically glued to his little girl.'

'I'm sure he's a wonderful father.' Rebecca refused to say anything negative that could be repeated.

'Come on or it'll be packed when the lunch crowd really hits.' Rae-Lynn grabbed her arm and dragged her inside. 'We all know Zac's close to being a saint but it sure is a shame.' She exhaled a sigh.

The temptation to discover more about him itched at Rebecca but she resisted.

'What do you recommend?' She steered the subject away from her itinerant musician.

'They're all awesome but I usually get one of the cast iron chicken tacos made with roasted tomatillo salsa, sour cream, cilantro and lime and another with fried tilapia topped with red cabbage, red onions, cilantro and a spicy dill yogurt. Plus a margarita, of course.'

'I think I'll steer clear of the margaritas today.'

'Lightweight,' Rae-Lynn teased. 'I'm only indulging because I'm off work.'

'What do you do?'

'I'm a civil rights attorney at one of the big law firms downtown.'

She quashed her surprise. Judgemental. Zac was right.

'Don't worry — it always shocks people which is why I love it!' Rae-Lynn's wide grin made it impossible for Rebecca not to laugh along with her. 'Let's join the line. We order at the counter then find a seat, and go back to pick up our food when it's ready.'

Already the place was filling up with an eclectic blend of customers. Workmen in dusty overalls chattered away in Spanish, boho students, musicians and smart-suited businessmen all queued up together. The decor could kindly fall under the heading of retro with its combination of wood-panelled and funky coloured walls, unmatched tables and chairs plus the occasional cactus plant thrown in for good measure.

'Susannah's obviously having a neat time in Cornwall. I can't get enough of her Facebook posts and Instagram pictures. We all love her to death and would've happily set the girl posse on Tom for the way he treated her.'

'The girl posse?'

'Yep, the three of us and Susannah are tight. I met her through work.'

Rae-Lynn flashed a grin.

'We could make you an honorary member in her place.'

Rebecca wasn't certain how to respond. She didn't want to come across as stuck up but she'd never done the close girl friendship thing well.

Luckily they reached the counter and the next few minutes were taken up with ordering. Rae-Lynn found them two seats on the end of a long table partly occupied by three giggling teenage girls busy taking selfies and pictures of their food.

'Susannah's been good to me.' Rebecca toyed with her drink, a delicious iced coffee made with horchata, a Mexican ground rice, sugar and cinnamon mixture she'd never heard of before. She gestured at her outfit. 'She even told me to wear anything I liked from her wardrobe.'

'She's a sweetheart.' Rae-Lynn found her smile again. 'That actually suits you better but don't tell her that.'

'Don't worry, I won't.' Rebecca laughed.

Romance on the Cards

'What did you do without me, Daddy? I told Ava's mommy you'd eat a frozen dinner and watch boring nature programmes on TV.'

So much for his reputation. Around his daughter there was no chance of getting a swollen ego. She wouldn't believe him if he admitted he'd gone out and Zac used that as his excuse to tell a white lie.

'You got me.' That's not a white one, dummy, it's a full blown whopper, he told himself. He set Harper's school bag down on the kitchen table. The next few hours would be the usual blur of homework, dinner, Girl Guides, bath and bed but Zac already longed for nine o'clock.

Instead of collapsing in front of the television he couldn't wait to get back to Rebecca's song. In his head that's how he saw it because without her the music would have no shape or form.

Last night he had worked until the early hours of the morning before finally falling into bed, exhausted. At eight he stirred briefly when Robin sent a text to say she'd dropped the girls off at school and he'd gone right back to sleep. He'd woken up to make the most of the quiet middle of the day. The melody and chorus were almost done but the lyrics were still causing him trouble. Tonight he'd tackle it again.

'You're not listening to me.' Harper's sharp protest jolted him back to real life. 'Ava's mom and dad are taking her to the aquarium in Chattanooga on Saturday and they asked me to go with them. Rosie's coming, too.'

'I'm sorry, sweetheart, but we're going to your grandma and grandpa's for Aunt Nikki's birthday. She's having a barbecue and all your cousins will be there.'

'Oh, Daddy, please,' she begged. 'Aunt Nikki won't mind.'

'I'm sorry but we've already promised Aunt Nikki and she'll be disappointed if we're not there.'

'I hate you. You never let me do anything fun!' Harper yelled and flounced out of the room to race upstairs and slam her bedroom door.

Zac glanced at his buzzing phone on the counter.

'You got X-ray vision, sis? We were talking about you.'

'No wonder my ears are burning.' Nikki laughed. 'I hope it was all good?'

'Depends on your point of view.'

'Spill the beans.'

'You'll tell me I'm a miserable old so-and-so too. You're always on Harper's side.' His half-hearted protest earned him a chuckle from his little sister.

Zac ran through the argument and sighed.

'She's got to understand you don't break a promise and especially not to family.'

'I get that, Zac.'

'But?'

'But I also know how important friends are to a girl,' Nikki ventured. 'Maybe you could compromise.'

'In what way?'

'You and Harper could offer to take me out for ice-cream on Friday night instead and you can come over to the barbecue as planned while she's out.'

He still saw that as giving in.

'I understand it's important to be firm with her, Zac, but sometimes you've got to bend a little.'

'In other words, pick my battles?'

'Yeah. She'll be a teenager before you know where you are and trust me, this is nothing compared with what you'll have to cope with then.'

'Is that supposed to cheer me up?'

'Not really.' She laughed. 'If it helps I assure you a gigantic hot fudge brownie sundae will soothe any hurt feelings I may or may not have.'

'You're a good kid.'

'Zacharias Quinn! I'm nearly twenty-five and own a successful business. Stop treating me like a baby.'

'Sorry.' He'd been ten when Nikki came along and the scrap of a baby with her sticking-up hair and piercing wail wriggled into his heart and never let go. 'All right, I give in. You knew I would.'

'Go and make peace with my sweet niece.'

'Sweet? I think you've been giving Harper 'woman' lessons.'

Nikki's wicked giggle trickled down the phone.

'I deny everything. Go and be a good dad.'

'I'm trying.'

'You're a great one. She's a lucky girl.'

Zac muttered something and hung up with tears pricking at his eyes. He shouldn't need reassurance but a rush of gratitude swept through him for it anyway.

★　★　★

Susannah's message popped in while Rebecca was poring through research on the training it took to become an opera singer, her main character's chosen career.

I'm discovering muscles I didn't know I had and I've only done a few of the shorter stretches of the path so far! Totally fallen back in love with Cornwall and I may never return to Nashville. Why didn't you mention your cute neighbour?

'Chris Tabb?'

Yeah, who else?

'I thought you were still heartbroken over Tom?'

Tom? I've consigned him to the Bad Choices Best Forgotten pile.

Rebecca envied her cousin's upbeat spirit although maybe they weren't so unalike. Travelling 4,000 miles obviously had given Susannah the distance to see things more clearly and was having the same effect on Rebecca in reverse. Comfort zones easily became ruts if people weren't careful.

I'm not treading on your territory, am I?

'Chris Tabb?' They'd grown up together and although he was a successful barrister and not bad looking these days Rebecca simply never thought of him 'that way'.

'Not at all. Best of luck. I expect updates.'

I hear I'm not the only one exploring the local attractions?

The girl posse. She should have guessed.

Rebecca pretended to misunderstand.

'I don't know how you stay slim living around here. The Pharmacy is incredible and today I went to the taco place for lunch.'

Good try, kid but we both know I'm talking about the super gorgeous Zac.

Rebecca needed to put the record straight before this got out of hand. Her reply gave an edited version of her encounters with Zac and put a heavy emphasis on the fact they probably weren't speaking to each other after yesterday's run-in.

You've got to admit life's more

interesting, though, now — right?

'That wouldn't be difficult.'

I'll let you off the hook for today but I'll check in again soon. Got to go. I'm cooking for Chris in the pursuit of improving transatlantic relations. LOL.

Rebecca stared at the blank screen and the title at the top of the page mocked her.

A Touch More Than Friendly.

Closing her eyes she conjured up Zac's gentle embrace before reluctantly running through their deteriorating conversation outside the house. She came to the conclusion that Zac on the defensive was no different from anyone else.

After losing her whole family in one awful night she'd buried herself in work, clung to her memory-drenched home and told herself and everyone else that she was coping. The last five weeks proved that to have been a big fat lie. Rebecca wondered if flowers felt this way when they started to bloom, blinking their petals against the sunlight and cautiously unfurling as they grew into the best version of themselves.

A tiny smile pulled at her lips. She and Zac Quinn weren't done. They'd only reached the end of Chapter One.

With the strains of the Countess's aria from the 'Marriage Of Figaro' playing in the background she got down to work.

Surprise, Surprise

'Heavens, Zac, you look like something the cat dragged in.'

'And here I was about to wish you Happy Birthday. Think I'll change my mind,' Zac quipped.

'Momma will throw a fit when she sees you. Haven't you slept in a week?'

If he answered truthfully she'd harass him but considering Nikki headed up the campaign to get him to refocus on his music he could blame everything on her.

He didn't realise he looked that bad until Robin Wingate had rolled her eyes when she saw him this morning and pleaded with him to go home and take a long nap.

'Sorry you couldn't make it for ice-cream last night.' He ignored Nikki. 'We'll reschedule next week.'

'We sure will. Suzy B's visiting her

folks today so we enjoyed our girls' night out earlier than planned.'

'I'm surprised you're up for more partying today.'

Nikki's raspy laughter exploded.

'Show your age a bit more. I'm twenty-five — not a dull and boring thirty-five-going-on-fifty. I've snagged a hot date tonight, too, with a really cute professional hockey player, so the weekend's just getting started. Come and get a beer.'

The rambling back garden of their old Quinn home swarmed with people, mostly their oversized family but with a few of Nikki's friends thrown in for good measure.

Nikki dragged him over by the back wall of the garage.

'Seriously, what's up? Are you ill?'

'I'm fine.' He laughed. 'I'm writing again, that's all, and time kind of got away from me. I sort of forgot the whole eating and sleeping thing.'

'Oh, wow — that's the best news I've heard in ages!' Her eyes shone. 'I'd like to bet a certain little lady inspired you. Am I right?'

'Listening to the Time Jumpers and seeing Andy Reiss again kick-started the old brain, I guess.' Zac ignored the veiled reference to Rebecca. 'I can't keep this up, though. Too much else goin' on in my life.' He tamped down a surge of disappointment.

'We'll see about that.'

This wasn't the time or place to argue the whys and wherefores of his complicated life.

'I'm starved. I hope Dad's got burgers ready.' Nikki poked his flat stomach. 'I hear it growling and pleading for food.'

She linked her arm through his and steered him towards the barbecue.

A few years ago their father got tired of trying to cook enough food for his growing family on a couple of normal-sized charcoal grills and competing with his wife for the small amount of indoor kitchen space. He designed and built an outdoor kitchen complete with a monster gas grill, a large charcoal one, sink, prep area, mini-fridge and bar.

'Talk about the lord of all he surveys.' Zac pointed to Seth Quinn, a beer in one hand and spatula in the other, flipping burgers and giving his vocal opinion on the Titans' non-existent chances of making the Super Bowl. 'He's in his element.' He glanced around. 'Where's Mom?'

'She's showing a couple of people round inside.'

'Oh, right.' He caught his father's eye and mimicked a drinking movement with his hand. 'I'll catch you later, kiddo.'

'Don't call me that, I'm . . . '

Zac smacked a kiss on her cheek.

'Yeah, I know, and I couldn't be prouder of you.'

⋆ ⋆ ⋆

'I love your home, Mrs Quinn,' Rebecca said as they made their way back to the front door.

'Call me Betsy, dear. It's Elizabeth really but Seth only calls me that when he's cross.'

They headed towards the garden and Rebecca stopped dead at the sound of Zac's distinctive deep laugh. When she accepted Nikki's invitation it had crossed her mind he might be here but she'd pushed it away and hoped . . . she wasn't certain what she'd hoped.

As he turned around and spotted her all the good humour drained from his face. Rebecca hoped no-one noticed and determined to stay well out of his reach. With a loaded burger in one hand and an icy beer bottle in the other she concentrated on not dropping either while she talked.

As soon as Betsy announced her as 'Nikki's cute little English friend' people had swarmed around her. Trying to sort them out wasn't easy but the three women closest to her age were married to Zac's older brothers.

She focused on the speedy ping-pong

of conversation and kept her back to Zac. Let him wonder what little titbits of news she might share with his family.

⋆　⋆　⋆

Zac could happily swing for his little sister. If he challenged Nikki she'd proclaim her innocence and say Rebecca was a friend so why shouldn't she invite her to the party. Why couldn't they all understand that at thirty-five years old he'd decide for himself if he wanted to date again? And if he did — a very big if — he'd select the lady himself.

Two could play the ignoring game.

'Hey, Rae-Lynn. How's it going?' he called over to Nikki's friend and she wandered across to join him.

'Hi, Zac. Where's Harper?'

'Gone to Chattanooga for the day with a school friend.'

'Let loose twice in one week? Careful.'

His jaw tightened.

'Not you, too. Give me a break.'

They'd known each other for years since Nikki and Rae-Lynn first started to rent a house together along with the voluble Suzy B. He usually enjoyed talking to her, possibly because there'd never been any spark of interest between them beyond friendship.

'Sorry. I didn't mean to get at you. Am I forgiven?' She playfully batted her eyelashes and he cracked a smile. 'That's better. Nikki tells me you're songwriting again.' Rae-Lynn poked his arm. 'Frowning doesn't suit you. If it was supposed to be a state secret you shouldn't have told your motor-mouth sister.'

They both loved Nikki but discretion wasn't one of her more obvious virtues.

'It's not a secret, it's . . . oh, I don't know. The whole thing's not goin' anywhere, put it that way.'

'You don't know that.'

'Yeah, I do.'

'Let's change the subject. Rebecca and I ate lunch at your favourite taco joint this week.' She gave a knowing smile. 'She didn't talk about you. In fact she very pointedly didn't talk about you, if you get my drift?' When he didn't respond she laughed and shook her head. 'You've both got it bad. Right now she's standing over there not watching you as stubbornly as you're doing her.' Rae-Lynn's emerald eyes shone. 'I could kiss you, if that would help?'

Zac nearly choked on his beer.

'You women have damn weird ways of solving problems.'

'Is that what Rebecca is?'

'Uh?'

'A problem?' She narrowed her gaze. 'I'm guessing you were a moron the other night.'

'Is that what she . . . ?'

'Gotcha.' Rae-Lynn's grin widened. 'She didn't in as many words but I'm not dumb. Are you going to apologise?'

'It's tricky.'

'Oh, Zac.' She sighed. 'Life's tricky. Surely you've worked that out by now. What I'm getting at is . . . I've never seen you look at anyone the way you did at Rebecca on Monday night. Everything about you softened and I thought she'd melt into a puddle of mush at your feet.'

He would have told her not to be ridiculous but his mouth wouldn't form the words.

'Yep, thought I was right.' Her voice held a triumphant lilt. 'I know there is a whole bunch of obstacles but you don't strike me as a quitter and neither does Rebecca. Go and make amends with our little Brit. She's worth it.'

'You're a good friend. The best.'

'Good luck.'

He suspected he would need it.

Alone at Last

'If I'm not breaking up anything important I'm taking Rebecca to see Dad's vegetables. She's a keen gardener and we were talking the other night about all he's got growing.'

Were they? Zac's pleading gaze made Rebecca's face burn. Dark rings circled his eyes. When had he last slept?

'If you're interested, that is?' The tired rasp lacing through his deep voice tugged at her jangled emotions and she couldn't refuse him.

'I'd like that.' Everyone around them tossed curious looks their way and she tilted her jaw in the air. Rebecca didn't have to explain herself to anyone.

'This way.' He gestured to let her go first and slid his hand around her waist. He silently steered them around the outside of the lawn until they reached a low white gate at the back of the garden. Suddenly he stopped and grasped her hands tightly.

'I'm sorry. Real sorry.'

'What for?'

'For everything,' he admitted with a lopsided smile. 'The way I spoke to you the other night. For being a prize idiot.' Zac nodded across the gate. 'And for lying about the vegetables.'

'You mean your dad doesn't grow vegetables?'

'Very funny. I mean the part about us discussing them and you being a gardening fanatic.'

Rebecca couldn't stop smiling.

'I actually do love gardens and grow all sorts of vegetables back in Cornwall.'

'Good. That makes me not such a liar.' He laughed and the same rogue strand of hair flopped forward. For the second time she couldn't resist brushing it away. 'I couldn't work out how else to get you away from my nosy family.'

'You do realise they're talking about

us now and trying to work out what's going on.' She hesitated. 'So am I.'

'Me, too, sweetheart.' His silky drawl sent shivers through her blood and unconsciously she shifted closer. Zac's arms wrapped around her and she leaned into his broad chest, surrounded by his tempting warmth.

'I could stay this way all evening.'

'But?'

'But I've only got an hour.'

'Before you turn in to Cinders again? You know, like in . . . '

'Hey, remember you're talking to the father of a Disney princess-loving girl,' Zac bragged. 'I'm an expert on the 'clock striking midnight and glass shoe' scenario. Harper is the reason I can't stay late.'

He explained where she'd gone and Rebecca silently thanked the family who'd given them this precious time.

'There's a bench near the compost heap where we can sit and talk.'

'Linking the words 'talk' and 'compost heap' is a trifle unusual but you've certainly got me intrigued.'

'And my family wonder why I don't have any luck with women!' Zac's dry response tugged loose another of the strings wrapped protectively around her heart. She'd never been a fan of men with big egos and he was genuinely oblivious to his undeniable charm.

'I'm here, aren't I? Or don't I count?' Her teasing response made him blush. 'Come on. Let's not waste any more time.'

'Hugging isn't a waste of time.'

'That's not what I meant and you know it.' Thank goodness there wasn't a mirror nearby because she could only speculate on the depth of her own embarrassment — somewhere between scarlet and fire-engine red would be her guess.

'Just wanted to hear you say it, honey.'

Every time his tempting drawl deepened Rebecca fought to hold on to any atom of common sense.

'Vegetables first,' he declared and let

go of her before seizing one hand again, engulfing it with his own.

'Vegetables?'

Zac's warm chuckle rumbled through his chest and lodged somewhere in the base of her stomach.

'A quick rundown in case you get interrogated later.'

'There'll be no 'in case' about it,' she muttered, pushing open the gate. 'Lead me to the cabbages.'

★ ★ ★

He'd been pumped up to sort things out with Rebecca but now Zac didn't have a clue where to start. He ran a finger idly over her bare arm and sighed.

'Apart from pining over me, why are you so exhausted?'

'You spurred me to write again. It doesn't fit into normal working hours.'

'Me?' Rebecca jerked away, her eyes wide with amazement. 'Whatever are you talking about?'

Aware of time ticking away he raced through the story.

'That's about it.'

'I'm guessing you were good?'

Zac shrugged.

'I sold a few and they did OK.'

'Are we talking ordinary OK or topping the charts OK?'

''Another Lonely Day' made it to number one,' he admitted. 'But the long hours and commitment took their toll. It helped drive me and Louisa apart.'

'You're saying the marriage would have survived if you'd given up your music sooner?' Rebecca probed.

'No.' Zac couldn't lie. 'We were fundamentally unsuited. I see that now. I thought having Harper might . . . ' His voice trailed away as he struggled to put it into words. 'Louisa warned me she wasn't good 'wife material', whatever that is, when I proposed. But I wouldn't listen. When she got pregnant I was ecstatic.'

'And she wasn't. But you ended up

78

with your amazing daughter.'

'I did.' He swiped at the moisture blurring his vision. 'No regrets.'

'You dropped music entirely?'

'Nope.' Zac shook his head. 'I take the occasional session musician gig. Mainly background work in one of the local studios. It pays the bills and keeps me somewhat in the loop.'

'Tell me about the song.'

'What song?'

She raised her eyebrows.

'What one do you think? The song that's left you looking like . . . '

'Something the cat dragged in?'

'Not quite how I'd phrase it!' Rebecca laughed. 'But very accurate.'

'Those were Nikki's words,' Zac confessed with a wry smile. 'Pithy, isn't she? The song's about you.' A delicate pink flush raced up her neck and settled on her cheeks. 'But I'm having trouble with the lyrics.' He pulled at the bags under his eyes. 'End result.'

'Oh.'

'Glad you asked?'

Rebecca gathered a breath, slowly exhaling.

'We won't ever really know each other if we're not honest.'

'I want to be.'

'Me, too.'

Zac touched a finger along her jaw line and wondered how she'd react if he kissed her. A shy smile crept across her beautiful features and Rebecca's sapphire eyes glowed in the last rays of evening sun. His last hope of resistance died as Rebecca slowly licked her bottom lip.

'Daddy, Daddy, I'm back!'

He jerked away and ended up with an armful of hot, overexcited little girl.

'OMG, we've had the best day ever and you should've seen the shark. He was ginormous and . . . ' She pulled back and noticed Rebecca for the first time. 'Who's she and why were you kissing her?'

Escape From Reality

Rebecca wouldn't argue semantics with a child. Personally she wouldn't call the brief brush of Zac's lips a proper kiss. Harper's furious glare sliced through her.

'This is Ms Tregaskas but you can call her Ms Rebecca. She's a friend of mine.'

The pint-sized girl stood her ground and folded her arms across her chest.

'You don't kiss your other friends.'

'I know but Ms Rebecca is . . . special.'

She wished she could tell Zac how much it meant to hear him speak up for her but didn't dare look his way.

'I want to go home,' Harper declared.

'Wouldn't you like to play with your cousins awhile?'

'No.'

Rebecca jumped up.

'I heard a rumour about birthday cake and ice-cream. In fact Nikki told me she'd ordered three kinds of ice-cream. Anyone interested?'

'That sounds . . . '

'I've eaten a ton of pizza and an enormous banana split,' Harper interrupted. 'If I have any more I'll throw up.' She tossed Rebecca a satisfied smirk.

Zac's resigned expression warned her about his decision before he opened his mouth.

'All right, we'll go now. You've had a long day and I think a nice bath and an early night is in order.'

'But I want to watch 'Beauty And The Beast' again,' Harper protested.

'If you're too tired to stay at Aunt Nikki's party that's not an option.'

Rebecca suppressed a bubble of laughter. Touché.

'Whatever.'

She watched his jaw tighten and sympathised. They obviously shared a mutual dislike of that overused word slung around by dissatisfied teenagers.

'Come on, Daddy.' Harper dragged at Zac's hand.

'By the time you run along and wish Aunt Nikki a happy birthday I'll be ready.'

'I want you to come with me now.'

Zac touched Harper's cheek.

'No answering back. I told you what we're gonna do.'

'Fine. Whatever.' Harper pulled away from her father and stomped off.

'Sorry about that,' Zac apologised.

'No need.' Coming between him and his daughter wasn't part of her agenda. 'You'd better go. I'll . . . see you around.' A tiny corner of her heart cracked open.

'That's it? See you around?'

She stared down at the grass under her feet.

'Be realistic.'

'I've been realistic for a long time, honey. It's not all it's cracked up to be.'

Rebecca needed to end this.

'Zac, if you're looking to give Harper

a stepmother I'm definitely not your woman.'

'A what? That never . . . '

'I'm not the maternal type and I love my single life.'

Zac shook his head.

'Either you're crazy or I am. How did we get from almost kissing to here?'

Your ten-year-old daughter who worships you and doesn't want any competition arrived on the scene, Rebecca thought.

She should thank Harper for jolting her out of a wonderful fantasy. Fairy-tale happy endings only happened in storybooks.

'I've got to go now.' He planted his hands on her shoulders, giving her little choice but to meet his uncompromising gaze. 'But one thing you may not know about me is that I always finish what I start.'

Before she realised his intention Zac moulded his mouth to hers and dragged them into a lingering kiss. He dragged one hand slowly down her back, spreading his fingers to press through her thin blouse before abruptly letting go.

'Enjoy the rest of your day.' He tipped an imaginary hat and strode off without a backward glance.

Rebecca's legs threatened to give way and she slumped back down on the bench. She touched her fingers to her mouth, running them over the imprint of Zac's kiss, and bit back tears.

★　★　★

While Harper went upstairs to take a bath Zac sprawled out on the sofa and ran over everything in his head. He'd expected too much of both Harper and Rebecca. Before today he'd kept any hint of a private life away from his daughter — rightly or wrongly — so she'd naturally been surprised and shocked. And Rebecca? No wonder she'd panicked. Their brand-new relationship wasn't strong enough to be tested.

'Daddy, I'm sorry I was mean.' Harper hovered on the bottom step, nibbling at her bottom lip.

Barefoot, in her pink flowery pyjamas with a halo of freshly washed curls framing her heart-shaped face, she reminded him of Nikki at the same age. Teetering on the threshold of becoming a woman while keeping one foot firmly in childhood.

'Come here, poppet.' Zac pushed himself up to sitting and opened his arms. She flung herself at him, her body shaking with loud sobs. He stroked her hair and didn't speak again until she settled down.

'I'm sorry, too.' Zac swore he'd always be honest with his daughter. 'I intended telling you I'd made a new friend but . . . I was nervous.' She fixed him with a puzzled stare. 'I really want you to like Ms Rebecca and be her friend.'

Harper bounced off his lap and plopped down next to him.

'You always say we're a team, Daddy.

We don't need anyone else!'

Zac tried a different tack.

'You and Rosie are good friends, right?'

'Yep.'

'And then Ava joined your class and now the three of you are all good friends.' Harper's wary expression wasn't encouraging but he ploughed on. 'Isn't it better to have two friends instead of one?'

'I suppose so,' she muttered.

'Would it be OK if I invited Ms Rebecca over for dinner one evening? You could meet her properly and she can get to know my special girl.'

'I suppose so.'

He'd take the grudging acceptance and not push any more tonight.

'Thanks, poppet.' Zac blinked back a rush of tears as Nikki's words filled his head.

'*When you're fifty and Harper's off living her own life what's yours going to be like? Pretty darn dull and empty, if you ask me.*'

'How about a bowl of popcorn and

the first half of 'Beauty And The Beast'?' He wagged his finger. 'Not the whole movie, though. It's too late.'

'And we watch the end tomorrow?'

'Deal.' He stuck out his hand and she playfully shook it. Tomorrow he'd negotiate with Rebecca. Zac suspected she'd need a bigger incentive than buttered popcorn and a Disney movie.

*   *   *

Maybe she should get angry more often. Talk about words flying across the page! At midnight Rebecca grinned as she allowed the first murder victim to be discovered. Her would-be contemporary romance had morphed into a psychological thriller with Mike Harding, a dark-haired American songwriter with a sultry Southern drawl, as her protagonist.

Her hands hovered over the keyboard and Zac filled her mind. Again.

'Ms Rebecca is . . . special.'

Harper's antagonism was no excuse

for Rebecca's bizarre accusation. As if Zac couldn't already have found a willing stepmother for his daughter, if that was what he wanted.

'How did we get from almost kissing to here?' he'd said.

She stared at the computer screen. At least here she directed her characters, a glorious relief from real life where nothing appeared under her control any longer.

Sound Advice

Zac ran a hand over his jaw and discovered his shaving job wasn't as good as he'd thought. Too late now. He ought to stay home and catch up with household chores before heading out to another assignment for Nikki but needed to do this before losing his nerve.

'Oh, it's you.'

What had he expected? For Rebecca to throw her arms around his neck and drag him inside?

Zac thrust the bunch of colourful tulips in her hands.

'I know it's clichéd to apologise with flowers but it's the best I could come up with on a Monday morning.'

'They're beautiful.' Her steady gaze melted a couple of degrees. 'You didn't have to do this.'

'Yeah, I did. I was a complete . . . '

'I believe idiot is the word you're searching for.'

'It is,' Zac admitted.

'I'm about to make tea if you'd like a cup? Or I've got instant coffee?'

'Tea would be good.' That struck him as the smart choice. Brits loved tea so maybe it would help his feeble case? He followed her in. 'Nice house. Whoever rehabbed this did a good job.'

'It was basically this way when Susannah bought it. She only repainted a few rooms. I love it, too, and I'll miss it when . . . I leave.' Her burgeoning smile faltered.

'Tea?'

'Of course.'

Zac picked up on her gratitude for not pushing the subject.

'Are you going for the wild cat look today?'

'Is it a bit much?' Rebecca frowned, tugging at the leopard print leggings she wore with a skinny yellow cropped shirt. 'I raided Susannah's wardrobe again.'

'Looks great.' Why did his eloquence

translate easily into music but desert him when faced with this woman?

A deep blush blossomed on her creamy skin as his eyes did the talking for him.

'Milk and sugar?' she croaked.

Zac nodded again, unable to risk speaking until he'd reined in his longing to kiss her again. The room shrunk and his awareness focused on her deep blue eyes and the hint of citrus swirling in the air between them.

She swung away and reached up to grab a mug from the shelf on the wall but fumbled it. Zac made a swiping catch with one hand and wrapped the other in a tight sweep around Rebecca's waist.

'Interception and touchdown,' he rasped. Zac nudged her hair out of the way and pressed a soft kiss on the curve of her neck. Rebecca gave him a quizzical glance over her shoulder. 'Football talk, honey. Real American football not your wussy soccer.'

'What are we doing?'

He eased her around and smoothed a loose strand of hair away.

'Having tea, I believe.' Zac grinned. 'Although I'd prefer a kiss but I'll take whatever's on offer.'

'I meant . . . '

'I know. Can we take this a day at a time and see where it leads us?' Zac strove to tell the truth without scaring her off. 'I don't know about you but I'm wary of putting myself out there again. I've been burned once and got the scars to prove it.' Rebecca turned chalk white. 'Hey, what's up? I thought you'd understand.'

'Oh, I understand all right. I suppose Susannah told Nikki.'

'Told Nikki what?'

'Don't insult my intelligence, Zac!'

'What are you jabbering about?'

Oh, heavens, he genuinely didn't know. Rebecca wished she'd kept her mouth shut.

'Are you going to explain or shall I leave?'

'Those are my only options?'

Zac shrugged.

'There's no point in being friends, or more, if we aren't going to be honest with each other.'

Of course he was right, but . . .

'Thanks for the . . . oh, that's right, we never did have tea.' Zac's borderline sarcasm wounded. 'You slipped up. Isn't that what y'all do? Drink tea and pretend everything's fine?'

She couldn't blame him for being angry but the idea of sharing the whole awful story made her stomach roil.

'I guess I'll see you around.' Having her own dismissal tossed back in her face shoved the knife in deeper. 'We could've had something good. I can't believe you're too much of a coward to tell me what's bothering you.'

Hot tears poked the back of her eyes but Rebecca refused to let them flow. Instead she stood there unblinking and allowed him to leave. The front door slammed, reverberating through the empty house and she slumped on to the counter. An eternity stretched out until she managed to lift her head again.

Methodically Rebecca went through the motions of re-boiling the kettle and making a pot of tea. She waited before pouring out a mug, splashed in too much milk and added a heaped teaspoon of sugar.

Swallowing a sob she tipped the tea down the sink, washed the mug and set it on the drainer to dry. On Saturday she'd poured her upset emotions into her writing so she would try the same remedy now. At this rate she'd have a bestseller written in no time at all.

Hours later she wriggled her shoulders and winced as her neck muscles screamed in protest. She'd come this close to killing off her hero but he'd argued her out of it, proving she needed to keep him or the murders would keep happening.

'I'm the only one who can save them — and you.'

Was she mixing up her book with real life? With her characters she often asked the question: what was the worst thing that could happen if they did or said a certain thing. The answer frequently dictated the direction of the story. Explaining to Zac about the fire would have roused his sympathy, the last thing she deserved.

Other people, Susannah included, didn't see it the same way. If she remained lonely and missed out on the prospect of love and a different kind of life, so be it.

★ ★ ★

Zac winced as the cold water ran over his bleeding finger. He should know better. Mixing a bad temper with a power drill could only end one way — badly. The jagged cut across his middle finger probably needed stitches but he was darned if he'd sit in an overcrowded emergency room for hours.

'Lord have mercy, boy, what've you done to yourself?'

'It's not as bad as it looks, Ms Barbara,' he tried to reassure the old lady. One of Nikki's most loyal customers, she always asked for him because on his first visit Zac had made time to sit down for a cup of coffee and a chat. Now there'd be a freshly baked cake waiting when he arrived — he'd smelled today's carrot cake the moment he stepped inside the door.

After cleaning the leaves from her gutters he'd spotted a broken kitchen chair in the garage and had offered to fix the leg.

'Have you got something I can bandage it up with?'

'I'll do it for you.' Barbara grabbed a clean towel and wrapped it around his finger. 'Hold it up in the air and go sit down before you fall down.'

'Thanks. I hope that won't gross you out too much?'

'I worked as a nurse for almost fifty years,' Barbara scoffed.

'I didn't realise.'

'No reason why you should.' Very efficiently she got him sorted out. 'Now you need aspirin, hot sweet tea and cake.'

Zac managed a weak smile.

'Never heard that prescription before.'

'It works wonders and afterwards we'll talk.' Her stern expression resembled his mother's when he wasn't being completely truthful. 'Don't fret, Zacharias. I'm not going to bite.'

He hand throbbed and he didn't have the energy to get up and leave so slumped back, cradling his injured hand and wishing he'd left the broken chair leg alone. And Rebecca.

'More tea?' Barbara held up the teapot and Zac remembered Rebecca and the tea they'd never got to drink.

'Um, no thanks. I'm good.'

'I doubt that. There's never been a man born who could make that claim with his hand on his heart.' The wry comment made him laugh. 'Tell me all about her.'

'Who?'

'The woman who got you tied up in knots, making you cut your hand half off.'

'Is it that obvious?'

'Yes. At least it is to someone who's lived eighty-five years.'

'Her name's Rebecca,' he said on a heavy sigh. Zac poured out the whole story. 'Any advice? Short of grovelling — that failed big time.'

'You rushed her and she wasn't ready to trust you. Something's bothering her and if you're patient she'll come around.' The old lady sipped her tea. 'When I used to work the night shift, people often opened up then about their fears. Something about the quiet darkness, I think.'

'You want me to sit at home with the lights out and hope she'll knock on my door to pour her heart out?'

'You young people take things so literally.' Barbara shook her head. 'What happens when you push Harper too hard?'

Zac's face burned. He'd confessed his failings as a parent more than once and there wasn't much this woman didn't know about his struggle to be a good father.

'She clams up,' he muttered.

'But if you give her what the modern

generation calls 'space'?' Barbara prompted.

'She tells me when she's ready.'

Barbara's satisfied smile verged on smug.

'I ought to be going. If it's OK I'll take your chair with me and finish fixing it at home.'

'When your hand's better.'

'Yes, ma'am.'

'Rest it for a few days and keep the wound covered for at least a week,' she warned and eased herself out of the chair. 'I'll keep one slice for myself but take the rest of the cake home with you. I'm guessing baking isn't one of your skills?'

'Definitely not.' Zac chuckled.

Out at the front door he and Barbara stopped for a moment.

'You're a good man, Zacharias. If I was thirty years younger . . . well, a bit more I suppose,' Barbara added, 'I'd snatch you up myself. I want to hear when your Rebecca comes to her senses.'

'You'll be the first to know,' he promised. Despite his aching hand Zac felt more upbeat. His improved mood lasted until he reached home and met the postman trying to deliver a registered letter from a Los Angeles attorney.

Zac read the legal prose several times. How on earth would he tell Harper?

Breaking Bad News

The warm breeze ruffled Rebecca's hair and for the first time in days a sense of peace settled around her. Not in the literal sense because noisy birds flitted around fighting to make themselves heard over the deafening roar of rushing water.

'Pretty impressive, isn't it?' Nikki asked, coming to stand by Rebecca on the trail.

After a long tedious week Rebecca had almost turned down an offer from the girl posse to go hiking at Fall Creek Falls state park, a two-hour drive from Nashville, but thankfully changed her mind.

'It's the highest waterfall in the eastern United States. If you're up for it we can hike down to the base of the gorge. We always came here on the Labor Day holiday at the end of August and went swimming in the plunge pool,' Nikki told her.

'I'd love to see it. Where did Rae-Lynn and Suzy B disappear to?'

'They're still chatting up a couple of medical students they bumped into.' She gave Rebecca a sideways glance. 'Everything OK? You seemed a little down when we picked you up.'

'I'm fine.'

'Hmm. If it helps any Zac's had a lousy week, too.'

'Why would that help?'

'Maybe because the two of you . . . '

'There is no 'two of us'.'

'If you say so.'

'I do.' Her unequivocal response earned Rebecca a hard stare.

'He cut his finger pretty badly on Tuesday.'

'Will it be all right?'

Nikki shrugged.

'I guess. Mother forced him to see the doctor but it was too late for stitches and seemed to be healing. It's still strapped up and he can't do much in the way of work.'

'I'm sorry.' Rebecca longed to beg for more details but held her tongue.

They walked along in relative silence and Nikki pointed out the different types of trees shading the trail, from giant oaks to hickory, tulip poplar and hemlock.

Rebecca got the distinct impression her friend was biding her time before raising the subject of her brother again. Reaching the Cane Creek suspension bridge they reverted to fun mode, grabbing on to the thick rope and wobbling their way across the river to reach firm ground again.

'I don't know about you but I could murder an ice-cream,' Nikki suggested. 'We can get one down at the visitor centre.'

'What about the others?'

'They'll catch up with us and then we can hike to the base of the falls together,' Nikki said. 'Come on.'

Rebecca didn't have much choice.

'Sounds good.'

Soon they'd bought their snacks and found a quiet spot to sit on the grass.

'Zac got some bad news a few days ago.'

Rebecca succumbed to a deep sigh. Her friend wasn't going to give up easily.

'Sorry, I thought you might care.' Nikki bristled.

'I do, but it's complicated.'

'Complicated is trying to find a way to tell his daughter that the mother she never knew died suddenly last month!'

'Oh, my goodness, that's awful.' She touched Nikki's hand. 'I honestly am sorry.'

'Yeah, I know. It sucks. I love Harper to death and this'll be so hard on her.' Nikki played with her ice-cream wrapper. 'The poor kid always hoped Louisa would come back for her.'

Rebecca's heart broke all over again.

★　★　★

Zac should have got this over with on Tuesday instead of letting it fester all week. He watched Harper munch her way through a loaded chilli dog.

'Aren't you hungry, Daddy?'

'Not really, sweetheart.' He pushed his plate away. 'There's something we need to talk about.'

Harper beamed.

'My birthday? You promised me a guitar and I want a sleepover party with . . . '

'Hang on.' Zac touched her arm. 'We'll talk birthdays soon but this is about something else.'

'I know I only got a B on my spelling test but I'll study harder next week, I promise.'

His daughter's earnestness touched Zac. Louisa would never know what a beautiful girl her baby had grown into. The occasional stroppiness and angry outbursts meant little in the long run because her good-hearted nature always rose to the top.

Zac swallowed hard. Keep it simple and be honest. His parents' advice kicked him into line.

'It's about your mother.'

'She's coming to see me?' A wide smile lit up her face and in that moment he'd have given anything to avoid breaking her heart.

'No.' As a newborn she'd fitted into one of his big hands and gazed at him with those same wide eyes. 'Your mommy got sick. Very sick. The doctors tried their best to help her but they couldn't and I'm afraid she isn't with us any longer.'

For several seconds Harper didn't speak.

'Do you mean she's gone to heaven like Grandma Patty?'

Zac nodded.

'I'm real sorry, sweetheart.' He'd been prepared for tears but Harper sat in silence, staring at the kitchen table.

'I'm going to my room, Daddy.' She pushed the chair back and stood up.

'Don't you want to talk?'

'Not now.' The curtain of childishness was stripped from her pale features and she left the room without saying another word.

Zac rested his head on his folded arms and gave in to his own grief.

⋆ ⋆ ⋆

Nothing struck Rebecca as the right thing to do after the way they'd parted, but to do nothing felt equally wrong. A sympathy card was the obvious answer but Rebecca needed to see Zac in person.

Outside his house she received a few strange looks from the driver while she texted and waited for a reply.

Nikki told me about Louisa. If you want to talk I'm outside.

Nothing.

'You'd better take me back . . . Oh, hang on.' Rebecca put the phone away.

Zac stood at his open front door, hands shoved deep in his jeans' pockets. She thrust a handful of money at the driver, thanked him and jumped out.

Smiling didn't seem appropriate so Rebecca raised her hand in a sort of half-wave. When his stony expression didn't alter her heart raced until she thought it would burst out of her chest.

Mentally setting herself up for rejection she strode up the paved drive.

Zac beckoned her in.

'Do you mind if we sit out on the back porch? I don't want to wake Harper.'

Close up she registered the air of heavy sadness etched into his face and ached for him.

'That'll be perfect; it's a lovely evening.' She followed him through the quiet house until they reached the kitchen.

'Mind the step down.' He opened another door. 'Make yourself at home and I'll be right back.'

Rebecca wandered on to the charming porch running the full length of the house, loving its simple rocking chairs, raffia flooring and plant pots overflowing with colourful yellow and purple pansies.

'Care to join me?' Holding up a

bottle of wine and two glasses he almost smiled. 'You'll save me from drinking alone.'

She nodded, settled in one of the chairs and clasped her hands on her lap.

He folded into the chair next to her and kicked it into a gentle rocking motion.

'All around I'd say this week is best swept under the carpet.'

'Will wine do the trick?'

'Nah.' He shook his head. 'Might dull the worst of the sharp edges, though. Sometimes that's all you can hope for out of life.'

'Doesn't sound all that different from drinking tea and pretending everything's fine.' Rebecca put her hand to her mouth. 'Sorry, I didn't mean to compare . . .'

'My ex-wife dying with whatever you wouldn't talk about on Monday?'

'Oh, Zac, I didn't come here to argue again.'

'How about telling me what you did

come here for? I could do with a laugh.'

His cynical response knocked her sideways and her mouth gaped open.

One Day at a Time

Zac could have kicked himself as Rebecca's skin paled to match the white paint.

'I'm sorry. I've no right to speak to you, or anyone, that way,' he apologised. 'Can we try again?'

'That's the story of our . . . whatever this is.' Rebecca's quiet rebuke sliced through Zac.

She reached across and stroked his bandaged hand.

'Start by telling me how this happened.'

Admitting he'd been juvenile and allowed his feelings to lead him into reckless behaviour wasn't easy but he stumbled through and waited to be rebuked.

'Oh, you silly man. Will it be all right?'

'Doc said so. Ms Barbara's a fine nurse.'

'Should I be jealous?'

He chuckled.

'She's a sweetheart, but I'm pretty sure she's not looking for a toy boy. Ms Barbara's eighty-five with snowy white hair, hearing aids and a walking stick.'

'You told her about me?' When he didn't reply immediately her laughter trickled through the warm air. 'She told you off.'

'Maybe.'

'What advice did she give?'

'To be patient and not rush you,' he muttered.

'Smart woman.'

He hadn't turned the lights on and the evening drew in on them.

'Ms Barbara said, when she worked the night shift, that was when patients would often open up. Something about the quiet darkness working on their fears.' Zac quirked a reluctant smile. 'I asked if she wanted me to sit at home with the lights out and hope you'd knock on my door.'

'Maybe we both need to thank her.'

'Yeah.'

Rebecca stared down at her lap.

'About ten years ago I lost my parents and brother in a house fire.'

'And you thought I knew?'

Quiet sobs wracked her body.

'Oh, sweetheart.' He pulled back up to standing and brought her along with him, wrapping her in a tight embrace. Zac absorbed her pent-up heartache until she had no more tears left.

'I came to comfort you, not . . . '

'Be comforted? It works both ways, honey.'

'Will you tell me about Louisa?'

Zac remembered Barbara's words and didn't press to change the subject back. He suspected she'd broken through a huge barrier by even mentioning the tragedy.

He sat down and immediately knocked back his drink.

'Make yourself comfortable. It's a long story.' A hint of resignation threaded through his voice. 'I went to college here in Nashville at Belmont University. I was studying music and she . . . ' Zac gave a wry smile ' . . . never studied much at all. She relied on her beauty to get her through.'

His expression hardened.

'I'm always telling Harper how smart and talented she is. I never want her to believe that her outside shell is all she amounts to. Louisa was the ultimate party girl and I stupidly thought I could pin her down.'

'Don't say that. You loved her.'

'In a way.'

'She treated you badly?'

'Oh, yeah.' Zac rubbed a hand over his jaw and sighed. 'My folks weren't thrilled when I proposed on graduation day but Louisa threw herself into the wedding plans and loved every moment.'

'Real life not so much?'

'You nailed it.' His bitterness made Rebecca wince. 'A tiny apartment and very little money wasn't Louisa's idea of a good time. Finding out we were having a baby didn't help matters because she felt trapped.' Zac explained. 'I thought, hoped, it would bring us closer. The moment Harper was born my world changed.' His voice lowered to a rough whisper. 'I never understood why Louisa's didn't, too.'

'She tried for a while?'

He shrugged.

'Sort of.' Zac's eyes clouded. 'But she didn't even hang around for Harper's first birthday.'

'Where did she go?'

'Los Angeles. With the same stupid dream as a million other pretty girls,' he scoffed. 'She'd make it big in Hollywood and show us all.'

'Did you hear from her much?'

'Nope. Not a word until I used a private detective to track her down. I filed for divorce a year or so later but we didn't even have to go to court because she didn't fight for custody of Harper.' Zac clicked his fingers. 'Like that, it was over.'

Rebecca tried to come up with a positive response but settled for taking hold of Zac's hand.

'I always told Harper a kind version

of the truth, but I never encouraged her to believe Louisa would come back.'

Rebecca could only imagine what went on in the little girl's head seeing all her friends with their mothers and wondering about her own.

'The worst thing now is that she won't talk to me about it.'

Zac's obvious anguish broke Rebecca's heart.

'She listened so quietly when I told her then went to her room. When she came down for lunch you'd think nothing had happened.'

The parallels with her own life ripped through Rebecca. She'd buried her broken heart along with her parents and Harry but she realised now that wasn't healthy.

'What am I going to do?' he pleaded. 'My mom's of the same school as Ms Barbara. Be patient, make myself available to talk and she'll come around in her own time.'

'I can see their point and hopefully they're right.' Rebecca needed to tread carefully.

'But?' he pressed.

'You might consider a grief counsellor who specialises in children.'

'Did that help you?'

'Me? I wasn't a child.'

Zac touched her face, barely skimming his finger over her cheek.

'Doesn't matter.'

'I didn't need ... I mean ... ' Rebecca dropped her gaze from his eyes, unable to meet the sympathy pouring from them.

'Sorry, does that come under the heading of 'mind your own business'?'

'Not exactly but I thought we were talking about Harper, not me.'

'Right,' he drawled. 'You're not gonna let me in, are you?'

'I'm not sure I can. Look, I really should leave now. You need to get some sleep.'

'More polite evasion. Is that an English thing or simply you?'

Rebecca pushed his hand away and reached into her bag for her mobile to make a quick call.

'I'll wait outside. My taxi will be here in ten minutes.' She considered trying to explain herself but simply couldn't.

Zac opened the door.

'I would give you a ride but I can't leave Harper alone.'

'I wouldn't expect you to.'

'We'll wait together for your cab.' His stern tone didn't brook any argument.

Outside the front door the silence was anything but comfortable.

'It might not seem that way but I do appreciate you coming over.' Zac's quasi-apology softened her resolve and she dared look at him again. 'We're an awkward pair.'

She wasn't sure about his word choice but somehow found herself cracking a smile.

'You can say that again.'

'We're an . . . '

'You are so literal, Zac Quinn.'

'Zacharias, if we want to be really literal,' he joked. 'By the way, are you always out-in-full Rebecca or does anyone ever shorten it?'

'Susannah and a few other friends call me Becky. Harry used to call me Becks.'

'Who's Harry?'

'Harry is . . . ' her voice wobbled 'was my brother, ten years younger than me.'

Zac reached for her hand.

'Doesn't it feel better to say Harry's name out loud than for him to be forgotten?'

Tears prickled at her eyes and she managed to nod.

'Another day you'll tell me more about him.' His quiet certainty touched something deep inside Rebecca.

A car drew up and the driver rolled down his window.

'Ms Tregaskas?'

'I'll call,' Zac promised.

'Good.' She reached up to kiss his cheek but Zac foiled her by turning at the last second. He cradled his hands around her face, threading his fingers through her loose hair and pulling her in for a swift hard kiss, laden with heat and promise.

'Goodnight, beautiful Rebecca.'

So much for a quick visit to offer sympathy. She must have been mad to think anything connected with Zac would be straightforward.

New Beginnings

Please come and fetch Harper as soon as you can. She's a bit upset.

The cryptic message from Paul Jones, Harper's swimming coach, made Zac abandon the song he'd been working on.

He hurried over to the pool and spotted Harper sitting alone on a bench, hunched over her bent knees.

'Hey, Paul, what's up?'

'Daisy Minor's mother put her foot in it. She didn't know Harper's story.'

'Story?'

The coach ran a hand over his stubbly grey beard.

'About her mom and stuff. Tina Minor was talking about going with Daisy to a mother-daughter dance at the Y next week and told Harper she should get her mom to take her.' Zac gave a sharp intake of breath. 'I'm real sorry.'

'Not your fault.' Zac hesitated. 'What did Harper say?'

Paul shrugged.

'Poor kid kind of lost it and lashed out at Tina, then she started crying and we couldn't console her. Tina felt awful when I explained.'

'I'd better take Harper on home.'

'Might be for the best. It's a tough thing for any kid to deal with.' Paul nodded. 'Tough for you, too. Harper's a great girl. She'll be OK.'

Zac needed to believe that.

'Go and take care of her. I'll give Tina a call later and put her mind at rest.'

'Cheers, Paul.' As Zac turned away Harper spotted him and her desolate expression ripped his heart out. 'Hey, sweetheart.' Zac eased the towel out of her hands and wrapped it around her.

'Oh, Daddy.' She sobbed and shivered in his arms.

'How about we go home? After you have a nice hot shower I'll make us some hot chocolate.' A miniature smile lightened her sad eyes.

'With marshmallows?'

'As many as you want, honey bee.' Zac slipped her flip-flops on her cold damp feet and picked up her swimming bag.

Usually on the way home from her activities Harper never stopped talking, but today she slumped silently in the back seat. He kept up a one-sided conversation and back at the house let her go upstairs without pressing any more.

'There you go. I couldn't fit in another marshmallow.' Zac set the overloaded mug down on the coffee table. 'Do you want me to comb your hair while our drinks cool down?'

Harper nodded and passed him the wide-toothed comb.

'I remembered to comb it before my shower and put on lots of conditioner like Aunt Nikki told me.'

Thank goodness for his sister. He hadn't thought too much about the future when he'd been left with a one-year-old girl to raise, and hair was only one small part of the equation.

Zac gently started at the bottom and made his way up to her scalp, letting out a breath when he succeeded without setting off more tears.

'I was mean to Daisy's mom.'

'Yeah, I know. She didn't mean to upset you but she hadn't heard about . . . your mommy.' He scrabbled around for the right thing to say. 'Would you like me to tell you more about her?'

Harper snuggled on to his lap, her hot chocolate forgotten.

★ ★ ★

Rebecca refused to turn into one of those women who sat around waiting for a man to call. Zac had a lot on his mind at the moment and she'd try to be patient.

The cathartic effect of writing helped and since Saturday she'd killed off one more character — a particularly unpleasant old man — and inched her reluctant hero closer to solving the mystery.

She'd also embarked on a programme of self-improvement, starting with an hour of yoga each morning. Rebecca painted her nails, exfoliated and moisturised every inch of skin and put herself in the hands of Susannah's hairdresser. Her building society colleagues wouldn't recognise her.

Strangely, with each passing day she hardly recognised her old life. Rebecca preferred the new version of herself.

Her phone buzzed and showed Zac's number.

'Are you busy or free to talk?'

'Well, I am reading a compelling book but I'll put it to one side if you promise to be witty and interesting.'

Zac chuckled.

'Not sure I can promise that. Sorry I didn't ring before.'

'Not a problem. I've been busy.'

'Killing more people?'

'If anyone's recording this conversation you'll get me in trouble.'

'Is that likely? Don't tell me you're on some sort of government watch list?'

For a fleeting second she wondered if they were right to crack jokes.

'Don't go all reticent on me. Yeah, I'm sad about Louisa but only because of our history and the fact she was so young. She wasn't the love of my life.'

'How's Harper?'

'She didn't have a great day.'

Rebecca hurt for the little girl as Zac explained what happened at the swimming-pool.

'You did the best you could.'

'You think so?'

'Yes, Zac, I do. You were there to comfort her and answered her questions.'

'Who was there for you?'

'No-one.' She blurted out the truth.

'I'm sorry.'

'That's life.'

'It doesn't have to be. I'm a good listener.'

But you can't wipe away my guilt, Rebecca thought. No-one can.

'I'm sure you've got a better reason

for ringing than offering me therapy.'

'You're an expert, aren't you?' A mix of annoyance and amusement threaded through his voice.

'At what?'

'Avoiding talking about difficult sub-jects.'

'Aren't we all?'

'Why are we always at odds?' Zac sighed. 'Of course you're right about why I called. Would you like to go with us to the zoo on Saturday?'

'The zoo?'

'Yeah, you . . . '

'Animals, birds, reptiles — I know. You're so sharp you'll cut yourself one day, as my granny used to say.'

'Very funny. So?'

'So?'

'Yes or no to the zoo?'

Rebecca wasn't sure about the wisdom of accepting.

'Harper's OK with me inviting you along.' Rebecca doubted that very much.

'Hey, I didn't say thrilled — simply

OK. I'm not lying to you.'

Zac always wrong-footed her.

'Fine. I'll come.'

'We'll pick you up at ten and grab lunch there.'

'Thanks.' They said goodnight and as she sat there holding on to her mobile Rebecca wondered if she'd made another wrong decision.

Animal Magic

Harper was smart. She'd cleverly realised Zac would agree to just about anything at the moment and negotiated the addition of Ava and Rosie to their zoo expedition.

That neatly scuppered Zac's plan to use the day as an opportunity for Rebecca and his daughter to get to know each other — he refused to count their first disastrous meeting at Nikki's birthday.

Zac disliked driving his mother's ancient Chevy station-wagon but used it because he couldn't fit everyone in his truck. The three girls giggled happily in the back seat as he stopped outside Rebecca's house.

'I'll be right back.' He jumped out and left the windows rolled down for some air.

'Wow! Is that your daddy's girlfriend?'

Ava's piercing voice followed him. 'She's pretty.'

'She is NOT his girlfriend,' Harper retorted.

Zac couldn't stop staring at Rebecca standing in her doorway.

'Aren't these jeans and shirt suitable?'

He grunted, finally processing her question.

'Yeah, you look . . . great.'

Gorgeous came to mind but she'd laugh if he said that out loud, and so would the gaggle of ten-year-old girls watching them. The white peasant style top decorated with tiny blue flowers and paired with dark jeans were fresh and simple. She'd also done something eye-catching to her hair but he didn't dare make any comment now.

'I'm sorry, but Harper talked me into bringing two of her friends.'

Rebecca grinned.

'We'll be well chaperoned.'

'Oh, yeah.'

She locked her door.

'Lead the way.'

'At least I get you up with me in the

front seat. They couldn't argue me out of that one.'

'Good.'

Zac opened the car door for her.

'Girls, this is Ms Rebecca.'

'I know. We've met.' Harper's sharp response deserved a reprimand but he remembered Nikki's advice about picking his battles.

'The other two young ladies are her best friends, Ava and Rosie.'

'It's lovely to meet you both.'

'OMG, you're English!' Rosie yelped. 'That is so cool.'

Zac caught Harper scowling. If the other girls took to Rebecca it would either help or hinder and he guessed they'd know by this evening. Concentrating on driving he let the conversation roll over him.

'This is so great. Now I don't have to put up with my stupid brother and sister all day,' Ava announced with a dramatic sigh. 'Do you have any siblings, Ms Rebecca?'

'Not now but I had a brother called

Harry who died.'

'How old was he?'

'Ten.' Rebecca's voice trembled.

'That's the same age as us,' Harper whispered.

'Yes.'

'I'm really sorry.'

Zac could have kissed his daughter.

'Thank you.'

'What was he like?' Rosie asked.

'I don't think Ms Rebecca . . . '

'It's all right.' She touched his arm and managed a faint smile. 'It's good to talk about him. Nobody should be forgotten.'

Something passed between them and Zac felt they'd climbed to the top of a mountain and seen the other side for the first time.

'He played a lot of what you call soccer and was really good. Harry loved snakes and chocolate ice-cream.' Rebecca laughed. 'He adored practical jokes and never failed to catch me out.' She clasped her hands together. 'I loved him very much and I miss him every day.'

Zac's eyes burned and he grasped the wheel tighter. Even the girls picked up on the atmosphere and fell quiet.

And Zac thought being open about feelings and emotions was so wonderful? Now she'd spoiled everyone's day.

'I've never been to the Nashville zoo. Why don't you tell me all about it?' Rebecca tried to change the subject and hoped someone would help her out. All three girls started to talk at once and she could have hugged them.

'The girls agree certain things are non-negotiable.' Zac's rumbling laughter soothed the last vestiges of her unease. 'First we walk the Jungle Loop to check out the zebra, ostrich and alligators. We make a slight detour to see the flamingos and then go to Critter Encounters for the giant turtles and alpacas. Last stop before lunch is the meerkats.'

'They're super cute, Ms Rebecca,' Ava piped up.

'After we've eaten we'll walk around what they call the Botswana Overlook and see the giraffes and rhinos.'

'Sounds amazing.'

'After that it's up for debate.'

'We've got to try the zip line,' Rosie proclaimed.

'But the jungle gym is more awesome,' Harper argued.

'We might have to do a coin toss to decide. There isn't time for everything. Harper, tell Ms Rebecca what we always do last.'

'The wild animal carousel. I've been riding it since I was little and I still love it.' She smiled at her friends. 'We all do.'

'Here we are, girls.' Zac slowed down and turned into the zoo entrance. As soon as he parked the girls leaped out of the car and raced off. 'You OK?' He squeezed Rebecca's hand.

'Yes, but I'm sorry if I . . . '

'Don't apologise. I drummed into Harper last night about the need to talk and not bottle things up, whether it's about her mom or anything else.' He fixed his gaze on her and for a few wonderful moments Rebecca forgot everything else.

'Works for you, too.'

'And you?'

'Yeah, and me, Little Miss Clever Clogs.'

'Daddy, come on, you're wasting time!' Harper knocked on the window.

'Yes, Daddy, you're wasting time,' Rebecca teased.

'I'll waste more time with you later,' he whispered before brushing a soft kiss over her cheek.

Later couldn't come soon enough.

★ ★ ★

Zac agreed to Harper's plea to eat lunch at the outdoor Snake Bites snack stand instead of in the Zoofari café. It wasn't a totally selfless move because then he could satisfy his own craving for pork barbecue, served at the adjacent TN BBQ Depot.

'That should keep them quiet for a few minutes.' He settled next to Rebecca at the picnic table with the girls huddled together at the other end, eating burgers and luckily paying the adults absolutely no attention.

'I bet they still manage to talk,' Rebecca joked.

'It's good to see Harper laughing and having fun again,' he mused. 'Worth every penny.' Zac shook his head. 'Well, almost. I sure as heck couldn't afford three kids at this rate.'

'They're exhausting, in a good way.' She stretched out her legs. 'Is it the African section next?'

'Yep.'

'I'm glad your coin toss came down in favour of the jungle gym.'

'You didn't fancy checking out the zoo from the air?' Zac chuckled. 'And I thought you'd be game for anything.'

'I would have had a go but I'm pretty sure your daughter wasn't up for it.'

'Well observed, Super Sleuth.'

'You fixed it!'

'Shush.' Zac pressed a finger to her mouth and winked. 'She's not a fan of heights. I know it . . . '

'But her friends don't?'

'Correct.'

Rebecca sneaked a quick glance at the girls and turned back to give him a swift kiss.

'You're an excellent father. Harper's a lucky girl.'

'I'm not sure I'd call losing her mother lucky.'

'You know I didn't mean that.' Two blobs of colour heated her cheeks. 'But there are worse things.'

This wasn't the time or place to pry further into her family history.

'Yeah, you're right again. Sorry if I put my big feet in it.'

'Haven't you finished eating yet, Daddy?' Harper shouted, rolling her eyes at her friends. 'We're done.'

'All right, let's go.'

For the next couple of hours they didn't stop. For someone who didn't have children of her own Rebecca amazed Zac by managing to keep track of three conversations while soothing scraped knees and bruised egos after the jungle gym took its toll on the girls.

'Carousel time, I think,' Zac announced. 'I promised I would have you all home by five.'

'That's too early,' Harper complained.

'No arguments, please. Don't spoil the day now.' He made a grab for Rebecca's hand. 'Come on, let's race them.' The reckless move clearly surprised her and her eyes lit up.

'You're on.'

They set off at a fast sprint and the girls raced after them screaming at the top of their voices.

'We should let them win.'

'Hell, no!'

He sped up, dragging her alongside him and they reached the carousel a good ten seconds before Ava.

'Goodness, I'm out of shape.' Rebecca dropped her head to her knees and gasped for breath.

'Not from where I'm standing.'

'Zacharias Quinn, you're impossible.' Her face flamed.

'That's been said before.'

Purposely he turned his attention back to the girls, sorting out who got to ride on which animal and buying tokens to pay for everyone. Zac spotted an empty panda bear and flamingo next to each other.

'Those are ours.'

She raised an eyebrow but didn't object when he lifted her on to the tall leggy bird.

'Next time we'll ride the same one so I can hold on to you. Much more fun.'

'I'm sure it will be.'

A tingle of anticipation ran through Zac as the elaborately carved animals started to move slowly up and down to the jangling music.

He just hoped he had the nerve to seize the ray of hope she'd offered with both hands.

When Tomorrow Comes . . .

This could become an interesting habit. Settled on Zac's back porch on a gentle spring evening with a glass of wine in her hand and the man in question smiling from his own rocking chair.

'Capshaw Elementary is gonna teem with gossip on Monday morning and by the end of the day you'll be either a sister to Princess Diana or an Oscar-winning actress from Downton Abbey.' His laconic drawl heated her skin. All day she'd fought the draw of him until Rebecca's defences were in shreds. 'Oh, you'll also be marked out as Mrs Zacharias Quinn, Mark Two.'

'Are you looking for an apology?'

'Hardly.' Zac chuckled. 'You've single-handedly ratcheted up my reputation and disappointed a whole bunch of women in one fell swoop.'

Rebecca sat upright, stilling the chair with her toe.

'They wouldn't be queuing up to date you if they knew what a . . . '

'Honey, I'm kidding.' His rich brown eyes gleamed. 'There's no queue. Trust me.'

'I can't imagine why not.'

'And why's that?' Zac leaned forward, his floppy hair shading his face so she couldn't quite make out his expression.

'Begging for compliments, are we?'

'Nope. The truth.' An embarrassing sense of awkwardness swept through her. 'You want me to spell out why I can't understand your lack of a queue of suitors instead?'

'Not really.'

'Are you certain?' Zac fixed his piercing gaze squarely on her. 'You know I'm attracted to you. I've never tried to hide it. You're beautiful and smart with a great sense of humour . . . at least most of the time.' The engaging grin re-emerged and she couldn't resist smiling back. 'I enjoy spending time with you and want to do it a great deal more.'

He cocked his head to one side.

'Are we on the same page or reading different books?'

Rebecca desperately wanted to be honest.

'I'm afraid.'

'You think I'm not?'

He snatched up her hands and pressed them to his chest, bumping his thudding heartbeat against her trembling skin.

'I wish I could change that you lost the people you loved most in the world but I can't. I won't spout the regular garbage about them not wanting you to live a closed-down life either . . . '

'You just did in a subtle way.' Zac chuckled.

'I'll put a mark against today's date on the calendar — first time I ever got called subtle.'

'How do you manage it?'

'What?'

She'd never fallen for an overtly charming man before but Zac's unawareness of his appeal was completely genuine.

He'd never seen the much-joked-about 'queue' because he stayed focused on his family and work to the exclusion of everything else.

'You don't allow me to sink into gloom.'

Zac shrugged. 'There's a marked difference between that and thinking seriously about things. Not many people get to flit through life in a happy bubble but that doesn't mean it's wrong to have fun.'

'I've had a lot of good days since coming to Nashville,' she confessed.

'Has today been one of them?' His breath warmed her skin and Zac pressed a soft trail of kisses down her neck. He slipped his large hands around her waist to pull her closer.

'Yes, on the whole.' Rebecca's normal urge to hold back faded away. 'I'll actually go for totally good. Talking about Harry was a painful good but I absolutely loved being with the girls.'

Zac took a chance.

'And me?'

'Good is a rather lame word.'

'You're a writer so come up with something better.'

'You are too. Help me out.'

'Excellent. Superb. Outstanding. Magnificent. Exceptional. Won — '

'All right, I get the hint.' Rebecca put a hand to her burning cheeks. 'You love embarrassing me.'

'We'll agree it's been a 'good' day all round. So, what about tomorrow? Do you have any plans?'

'Tomorrow?' My only plans involve sleeping late and doing laundry.'

'My folks have a family open house on the first Sunday of the month. Come and join us. It'll be crowded and noisy but fun.'

'Are you sure? What about Harper?' A frown creased her brow.

'She'll learn, given time.'

A touch of wariness shaded her pretty blue eyes.

'I don't want to cause any trouble between you.'

'I understand that but Nikki berated me a few weeks ago and you did, too, about not centring my life around Harper to the exclusion of everything else. I'm simply following y'all's advice.'

Rebecca laughed.

'My goodness, no-one can toss my own words back at me quite the way you do.'

'I guess I'll take that as a compliment.'

'All right. I'll say thank you for the invitation and accept.'

'Great. I suppose we ought to get you home.' He struggled to be sensible. 'It's been a long day.'

'But a 'good' one.' Rebecca teased. 'One might even say stupendous.'

'Oh, one might.' Zac faked an English accent and received a smack on the arm.

'For heaven's sake don't ever try that again. Stick to song writing and leave acting to the professionals.'

'I'm happy to agree as long as I get a satisfying goodnight kiss.'

'Placing demands now, are we?'

Zac didn't fall for her lame attempt

to sound cross. He laughed and swooped in for a long lingering kiss.

'Did that help?'

'I might need another to be absolutely sure,' Rebecca whispered against his mouth.

She slipped her fingers through his tousled hair and twined them around the back of his neck.

'My turn.'

Her kiss lit him up from the inside out and Zac groused when she let go.

'Spoilsport.'

'There's always tomorrow.'

He didn't dare ask how many tomorrows they might have. Life didn't come with guarantees and theirs had the length of a 90-day tourist visa hanging over it.

'At least until the middle of June.' Rebecca's false brightness pained him. 'Let's see how things go, OK?'

Heart to Heart

Rebecca stared at the computer screen as her cousin stretched out in Rebecca's own brass bed in Cornwall, lazing away her Sunday morning with the familiar pile of white lace pillows tucked behind her head and her favourite print of Holywell beach visible on the wall.

'Are you always this sensible?' Susannah complained. 'You've been handed the chance for a new kind of life on a platter so for heaven's sake don't blow it.'

'I'm not,' Rebecca protested. 'My writing's going great. I don't care if no-one ever sees it because the satisfaction is immense. I promise I'm never going back to the building society.' A huge weight lifted from her shoulders as the words tumbled out. 'I'm not sure what I will do to pay the bills but that's not my main problem right now.'

'And Zac is?'

'It's not straightforward,' Rebecca hedged.

Susannah picked up a piece of toast from the small plate balanced on her bedside table.

'Nothing is.'

'You might be right. How's the coastal path these days? Have you got much further around?'

'Um . . . not really. I've been a bit distracted.'

'By a certain Mr Tabb, by any chance?'

'Maybe.'

'Are you two getting serious?' Rebecca couldn't imagine how they'd make the relationship work long term, any more than picturing her and Zac doing the same thing. 'You know Chris will never leave Cornwall and can you seriously see yourself giving up your life here?'

'Can you seriously see yourself returning to your life here?' Susannah threw the question right back.

'I told you — I'm going to change my job.'

'What about the rest of it?'

'You didn't answer my question!'

'Neither did you.'

Growing up they'd argue back and forth all day until it drove their families mad.

'Fine, I'll go first,' Susannah offered. 'I'm not dumb and neither is Chris. We know it's early days but we've talked about where we see this going and . . . let's say we're looking in a similar direction.'

'And that is?'

'Being together, in whatever shape or form that takes.'

'Wow! You don't hang around.'

Susannah laughed.

'We're not getting any younger, kid. Are you going to talk about what's going on with Zac?'

Rebecca launched into the whole story before she lost her nerve.

'You seriously said he 'affected' you? You're not Jane Austen. Get real, Becky.' Her cousin leaned closer to the screen. 'How can you not snatch every good moment you're offered?' she asked. 'I know you never want to talk about your folks and Harry, but . . . '

'That's right, I didn't, but now I realise that's ridiculous.'

'Finally!' Susannah clapped her hands. 'I knew I liked Zac for a good reason apart from the fact he's super cute.'

Rebecca didn't bother to argue.

'By the way, Lila did a great job on your hair. It's adorable. Have you raided my wardrobe yet?'

She didn't wait for a reply.

'I hope so because no offence, Becky, but your stuff here is hideous. I can't believe any thirty-something career woman dresses in the things I've found hanging up. They must be hangovers from the eighties!'

'My clothes aren't that bad, but I'll admit I've borrowed a lot of yours.' Rebecca sighed. 'And yes, they're a lot more fashionable. I promise I won't go back to dressing drearily, either, when this is over.'

Susannah beamed.

'I'd no idea my brainwave would turn

out so well. You're writing the next bestseller and we've both found love. I'd say I deserve an A-plus grade.'

'You do exaggerate. A bestselling book is as likely as winning the lottery jackpot. You might be in love, but with Zac it's . . . '

'Not straightforward. You already spouted that garbage.' Susannah smirked. 'Keep telling yourself that and one day it'll simply knock you on the head and you'll wonder why you were so stupid.'

'I have to go.' Rebecca ignored the gibe.

'Sunday lunch with the family?'

'Yes.'

Susannah frowned.

'So you need something smart enough to impress the parents but comfortable for hanging around with a bunch of kids. I've got it.' She snapped her fingers. 'Wear the blue and white striped shirt-dress with the three-quarter sleeves and flared skirt. Make sure you stick on the wide navy leather belt to cinch in the waist. What size are your feet?'

'An English size seven. Why?'

'Perfect. There's a new pair of navy low wedges stashed in a box in the right hand side of the closet.'

'I can't wear your new shoes!'

'You certainly can. And will.' Susannah grinned. 'That should kick Operation Zac into high gear.'

'Operation . . . ? Oh, fine, I give in.'

'Good. Now go and pretty yourself up.'

'What are your plans for the day?'

Her cousin tapped the end of her nose.

'That would be telling. Check in with me again tomorrow. Bye.'

The screen went blank before Rebecca could even say goodbye.

★   ★   ★

Zac checked his watch again. Nikki always rolled in late for lunch but today he'd asked his sister to pick Rebecca up on her way so as not to push his luck with Harper.

His mother yelled out of the back door at the children for them to get inside and wash their hands. From Noah's oldest — fifteen-year-old Trey — all the way down to Lucas's toddler daughter they'd disappeared into the garden earlier for an exuberant game of hide and seek.

Zac struggled to get his head around Rebecca's solitude.

Susannah and her parents appeared to be her only family and they weren't close on the same level as the Quinn clan. If she made settling in England a condition of being together how would he deal with that?

'Hi Momma, I'm early for once.' Nikki breezed in. 'I hope you're impressed.'

Zac craned his neck but couldn't see Rebecca.

'Don't fret. She didn't bail on you. Lucas was outside kid-herding and buttonholed her as soon as we got out of the car.'

'Wonderful,' Zac grouched.

'What did you expect? She's tough. She'll survive the gauntlet. Don't worry.'

As the door crashed back against the wall the decibel level in the kitchen soared. In reality there were only seven children but they made enough noise for 20. He spotted Lucas and Rebecca bringing up the rear and waved but Harper tugged on Zac's arm.

'Daddy, I don't feel good,' she whined and clutched her stomach.

'Why don't you go lay down on Momma Betsy's bed for a while? See if it passes off.'

'I want to go home.'

His mother came to join them and frowned at her oldest granddaughter.

'What's up with my poppet?'

Harper repeated her complaint and clung on to him.

'Come with me and I'll fix you some flat ginger ale and crackers. That'll settle your stomach. It's a shame you're feeling poorly because I've made your favourite pot roast today.'

'You did?'

'Can't you smell it?' His mother winked over Harper's head and Zac caught on to his daughter's devious ploy.

'That's a real shame,' he agreed.

'It's not as bad now. Maybe I ran around too much,' Harper suggested. 'I could try to eat a little.'

Zac shook his head.

'I'm not sure. What do you think, Momma, is that a good idea?'

'If she sits by me I can keep an eye on her.' Betsy put her arm around her granddaughter.

He stifled a smile as Harper grudgingly agreed. She knew she'd been rumbled. His mother whisked her off to wash her hands and chivvy the rest of the family to get to the table. Or rather tables, because with 18 to feed it took three these days.

'Is Harper OK?' Rebecca appeared by his side. 'She seemed fine outside.'

'I suspect it's a touch of the green-eyed monster.'

'Of me?'

'I think so.' Zac cracked a wry smile.

'But yesterday we got on well!'

'I guess I'm used to the mood swings of ten-year-old girls.' He chuckled. 'Nikki reckons it's getting me into practice for when she's a teenager.'

'I don't want to cause . . . '

'Quit saying that.' Zac pressed his fingers against her soft mouth, shiny with something deep pink and glossy. He couldn't forget how warm and sweet she tasted last night and wished they weren't surrounded by his large nosy family so he could check it out again. 'Momma will take care of her.' He tucked her arm through his. 'You're sitting by me.'

'I am?'

'Is that a problem?'

Rebecca's eyes shone.

'No. Remind me later to tell you about my conversation with Susannah.'

'Is she on my side?'

'I didn't realise there were sides but yes, she's definitely Team Zac.'

He laughed.

'I knew there was a good reason I liked your cousin.'

'Sit down or you won't get fed.' Seth Quinn's voice boomed out from the dining room.

Zac yanked out the two nearest chairs.

'Sit down and stake your spot and mine.'

'Where are you going?'

Zac caught a note of anxiety in her voice and ran a hand over her shoulder. Later he'd tell her how beautiful she looked in her fresh blue and white dress but right now she needed reassurance.

'It's OK. I'll be back. We all have allotted tasks and my job is to fix the drinks.'

'Can I help?'

'Thanks, but no thanks.' He tapped his father's arm. 'Look out for my lady.'

Her cheeks flamed a bright stoplight red at his casual claim and Zac bent down to brush a soft reckless kiss on her cheek.

The affectionate gesture would be noted but he didn't care. Let them say what they wanted. Only one person really needed to know and she stared wide-eyed at him.

No Easy Answers

My lady? Was Zac utterly mad? Why didn't he simply advertise his feelings on a flashing neon sign for everyone to see?

'Don't fret. Most of them are too busy to notice my crazy son.' Seth patted her hand.

At Nikki's birthday Rebecca instantly had liked the friendly man who'd welcomed her unreservedly. There was no doubt from where his four handsome sons inherited their good looks. The vigorous seventy-one-year-old's kind brown eyes still sparkled with life and she'd watched him run after his grandchildren like a much younger man.

'It only takes one,' she quipped.

'True. Uh-oh. Mama Bear at six o'clock.'

Rebecca glanced towards the kitchen

door and stifled a groan. Zac's mother's stern expression wasn't one of unbridled delight. She'd been perfectly amiable at the barbecue so why was Betsy Quinn giving her the evil eye now?

Harper was glued to her grand-mother's side and gave Rebecca a satisfied smile. What was the girl up to?

'My Betsy's been nagging me for years to take her over to Europe and I guess we ought to go before we're pushing up daisies. What's Cornwall like?'

Rebecca appreciated his attempt to ignore his wife's obvious displeasure and played along, checking out of the corner of her eye for Zac while she chattered away. Carrying a large tray, he made his way around the room delivering drinks and cracking jokes.

'Earth to Rebecca?'

A large hand waved across her face and she registered Seth's worried frown.

'You all right, hon?'

'Fine.'

'He's his own man.' He kept his voice low so no-one could overhear. 'They all are. Sure, they love the rest of the Quinn gang, but they've got their own lives.'

'Why are you telling me this?'

Seth selected a large dill pickle off a relish plate and crunched on it before answering.

'In case your mind's workin' overtime, and thinking along the lines of me and Betsy keeping them on a tight rein.'

Rebecca's face heated.

'Zac's doing a darn fine job raising Harper and we're proud of them both.'

'You're right to be,' she said. 'She's a lovely girl and Zac . . . is a good man.'

Seth's rumbling laughter made the family members seated nearest them look but luckily Betsy and a couple of her daughters-in-law had started to place platters of food on the table. Thick slabs of steaming beef, glistening vegetables, huge bowls of fluffy mashed potatoes and fragrant yeast rolls immediately took away their attention.

'Nothin' wrong with 'good', but fifty years ago my sweetie would have described me a lot more specifically.' He winked. 'I'm darn sure she would even now.'

Another hot blush raced up her neck.

'You're Zac's father. I'm hardly likely to tell you I . . . fancy him, am I?'

'Aw, sugar, it's obvious, and there's nothin' wrong with that.' Seth's gaze darkened. 'The boy hasn't had it easy. We all rallied around to help but at the end of the day the responsibility's all been his. He's given up a lot for Harper.'

'Willingly, I'm sure.'

'Yeah, but I'd be happy to see him with more joy in his life.'

Rebecca hesitated.

'I'm only here for another six weeks or so, Mr Quinn.'

'That's probably why she's fussing.' Seth gestured towards his wife. 'Betsy can't stand to see one of her babies hurt.'

'And you?'

'You've given Zac something priceless. Hey, you aren't eating.' He picked up a loaded platter. 'Help yourself.'

Rebecca started, confused by the sudden U-turn in the conversation.

'What are you two in a huddle about?' Zac levered into his seat while balancing three glasses. 'Sweet tea for us guys and lemonade for you.' He gave Rebecca hers first and shoved a drink across the table to his father. 'Please tell me you didn't bore her with the story of my pants splitting open in the middle of a school play?'

'Not guilty.' His father grinned. 'Let's eat before the food gets cold. Your mother won't easily forgive us that.'

Zac dropped his questions for now and got busy with enjoying the meal.

'If you're done, bring your dishes into the kitchen and get dessert.' Betsy stood and clapped her hands.

'Let's grab something we can sneak outside,' Zac whispered.

'What about Harper?'

'Fully recovered and totally disinterested in us. In a few minutes she'll disappear upstairs with Aaron's twin daughters. Trish and Tara are a full six months older than Harper and experts on all girly things, according to my sweet daughter.'

He managed to swipe a couple of brownies, steer them through the mass of people fighting over the various sweet treats on offer, deflect several attempts to engage Rebecca in conversation and navigate their way towards the back garden.

'Time to check out the vegetables.'

'You're such a romantic,' Rebecca teased. 'Is winning women over with carrots and green beans your prize strategy?'

Zac stopped halfway across the lawn. 'Am I succeeding?'

'I suspect you are. Much against my better judgment.' Another mischievous smile pulled at her lips.

'Come on before anyone spots us.' They sneaked off and settled happily on their favourite bench out of sight of the house. 'I totally get now why Dad spent so much time here when we were growing up. Must've been the only place he got any peace and quiet.'

'It's working for me. I love it.'

Zac bit back the response he got close to saying out loud.

'Good.' He waved the brownies up in the air. 'Good girls who tell the truth get the largest piece.'

Rebecca playfully ran her fingers through his hair and nuzzled his cheek.

'And what do bad girls get?'

'In trouble,' he growled and seized a quick kiss. 'What did my daddy have to say for himself?' Zac watched her brain cranking. 'The complete truth. No sugar coating.'

Why could nothing be simple? Sitting here in the warm sunshine next to Zac would be heaven if only she could push away all the negative thoughts. Rebecca attempted to sum up the conversation and did pretty well until she came to the part about admitting she fancied him.

'That's hardly news.' He flashed a satisfied grin. 'Come on, sweetheart, I know you do. I assumed you didn't go around kissing random men that way. If it's any consolation it's the same for me.'

She nodded, not quite looking at him.

'I mentioned the short time I'm going to be here but your dad didn't finish answering me when you turned up.'

'There's something more, isn't there?' Zac persisted, setting the brownies on the arm of the bench and wrapping his warm hands around hers. 'Is it Momma?'

Rebecca gave up.

'We caught her giving me a very unhappy stare.' She omitted any mention of Harper.

'Why? She likes you.'

'Your father took a guess that she's worried you'll be hurt when I return to Cornwall.'

He gently caressed her cheek.

'I didn't get around to telling you how beautiful you look today.' The abrupt change of topic confused her. 'I love your new hair thingy and the dress is . . .'

'My cousin's.' Rebecca couldn't help smiling. 'The new hair 'thingy' is courtesy of Susannah's hairdresser, in case you were thinking of getting a similar style yourself.'

'Hell, yeah.' Zac plucked at his tousled locks. 'Don't you think it would suit me?'

Rebecca laughed.

'I'm not being obtuse and ignoring what you said about my mom,' he went on. A shadow settled over his face. 'Dad was right when he said you'd given me something and I can guess how he planned to finish the sentence.' The break in his voice shook her. 'Dad mentioned joy but equally important is hope. You feel it, too. I know you do.'

Rebecca couldn't argue with him.

'You've overcome a ton of obstacles and so have I. None of this is insurmountable, honey.'

'I want to believe you.'

He planted his hands on her shoulders.

'Then decide to, and don't let

anything deter you.'

'Is it that easy?'

Zac shook his head.

'Is anything worthwhile ever easy?'

When she didn't reply he kissed her, wiping out any hope of making a sensible rational decision. She refused to spoil the wonderful moment by discussing Harper.

'You're right.'

A wide smile split his face in two.

'That smart observation earns you both brownies.'

Rebecca snatched them from his hands and took a large bite of the first one.

'Totally worth it,' she mumbled through a mouth full of thick fudgy brownie, loaded with nuts and topped with a delicious dark icing that she could happily eat with a spoon. 'This is divine.'

'So are you.' The throwaway compliment stopped her mid-chew. 'I'll talk to Harper tonight. It's time I was upfront about how much you mean to me.'

She refused to ask for any more details. They'd cope with the fallout tomorrow, because Rebecca didn't doubt there would be repercussions.

For now she'd relish this window of hope. Holding out the other brownie to Zac she cocked a smile.

'I'll share. I'm nice.'

'Oh, I know that.'

They munched on the gooey cakes, safe in their own little bubble of happiness.

On Bended Knee

'And you believed that?' Zac shoved a hand up through his hair and glared at his mother.

'Keep your voice down, son.'

'Why should I?' He turned on his father. 'You stood up for me at lunch. What's made you change your tune?'

Seth shuffled awkwardly from the kitchen sink over to the refrigerator, pulled out a soda and drank half of it down in one swallow.

'Your mother's right. You don't know much about Rebecca.'

'Who put this particular little worm in your ear?' He switched back to his mother, unable to let this go.

Reluctantly he'd watched Rebecca leave with Nikki, only after she'd promised to have lunch with him tomorrow.

'That's between me and them.'

'Garbage!' Zac spat out the word.

'I've a right to know who's maligning the woman I love.'

'Love?' Betsy scoffed. 'You haven't known her five minutes. For Harper's sake I expected you to be more cautious.'

'You and Daddy got married after knowing each other six weeks!'

'Please tell me you haven't proposed?'

'Of course I haven't.'

He folded his arms because it was either that or slam his hand on the table.

'I don't get it. After Rebecca came for Nikki's birthday you called her a lovely woman and when I said I'd invited her for lunch today you grinned from ear to ear.' Zac shook his head.

'What do you know about her brother's death?'

'Her brother?' His head reeled. 'Not a lot. He died in a house fire along with Rebecca's parents.'

'And why hasn't she told you anything more? Wouldn't that would be normal for two people supposedly 'in love'?'

The sarcastic emphasis on the last

two words cut through Zac.

'It's hard for her to talk about.'

'Perhaps because she's burdened with guilt.'

'Guilt? What for?'

Betsy shrugged.

'I don't know the details but someone questioned the circumstances around the tragedy.'

'So this mythical person, who you refuse to identify, spouted an unproven suspicion and you decided to believe that rather than ask Rebecca outright?'

A rash of heat mottled his mother's face and neck.

'You've always insisted on us not judging people, especially without knowing all the facts. I don't get why suddenly it's OK?'

'Maybe your mother overreacted.' Seth tossed an apologetic smile in his wife's direction. 'But she did it out of love.'

'Which makes it OK?' Zac yelled. 'I don't think so. I'm taking Harper home.'

'Don't be like that, son.'

He brushed off his father's attempt to touch his shoulder.

'You can defend Momma all you want but I'm not staying to listening to this rubbish any longer.'

Zac slammed the kitchen door behind him and didn't stop when Noah and Aaron glanced up from watching baseball.

'Harper, down here now, please!' he shouted up the stairs.

'Don't take it out on the kid,' Seth pleaded, catching up with him. 'She didn't mean any harm.'

'What do you ... ?' The penny dropped and Zac stared at his father. 'Harper told Momma that cock and bull story?'

'I never said ... '

'You don't need to. It's written all over your face.' Despite everything he managed a sad half-smile. 'You've never been able to lie well, Daddy. It's one of the reasons Momma loves you. That and your unswerving loyalty, no matter what she does or says. Most of the time that's a huge plus but today . . . ' Zac shook his head.

'Daddy, please can we stay longer?' Harper skipped down the stairs and his heart gave a painful squeeze. 'Trish, Tara and I are going to watch 'Frozen'.'

How could he tell her off? But how could he not? She needed to understand the trouble her careless words caused.

Sure, she was jealous of Rebecca, but that was no excuse. Except, maybe when you were almost eleven and afraid of having your world turned upside down, it was?

'Not today, sweetheart. You've got your art project to finish and I need to do laundry or you'll be going to school naked.' Zac made a joke of it and his father's worried frown faded. 'Run around and say goodbye to everyone while I see if your grandma's got any leftovers for us to take home. I bet she's got one of your favourite brownies tucked away.' A pang of disappointment hit him as he remembered Rebecca licking the soft icing from her lips and laughing.

'*None of this is insurmountable, honey.*'

'*I want to believe you.*'

'*Then decide to and don't let anything deter you.*'

'*Is it that easy?*'

No, it wasn't that easy, and at thirty-five he knew better.

★　★　★

Rebecca immersed herself in work, trying to see her latest murder victim — a naïve teenage girl with no apparent connection with the other victims — through her protagonist's eyes. Now she truly understood authors who claimed to lose themselves in their writing, because a few hours mired in imaginary blood and difficult characters who didn't always do what they were told was proving the perfect antidote to her jumbled-up brain.

Is anything worthwhile ever easy?

Everything came back to that particular question but the answer wasn't a straightforward yes or no. No matter how deeply Zac loved her, Rebecca accepted that Harper came first and in a toss-up between the two of them she'd — quite rightly — lose. She couldn't erase the girl's borderline-smug expression from her mind and puzzled about what caused the turn-around.

The two steps forward they'd taken at the zoo went into a complete retreat today when Harper totally ignored her. Maybe Ava or Rosie had said something to give Zac's daughter second thoughts.

Her phone pinged with an incoming message. Zac.

Rebecca's spirits lightened. They loved chatting late at night and she was too tired to write much more anyway.

Sorry. Got to cancel lunch tomorrow. Will be in touch. Z.

The curt message made her frown. Of a necessity texts were brief but even a single smiley face after his name would have made Rebecca feel less . . . rejected.

No problem. Talk soon. R.

Covering up the hurt came easy after all her years of practice. Sleep would elude her now but her book would benefit. Her hero needed some torment in his life — it was time to turn the screws on his past and make him beg for mercy . . .

A sharp pain stabbed into her right shoulder and Rebecca groaned, struggling to open her eyes. She cautiously stretched and raised her head from the desk before wiggling her neck from side to side.

The blinking icon on her computer showed several attempts by Susannah to video chat and she focused on reading the time in the corner of the screen.

Three thirty in the morning.

Are you there?

Another message popped in.

Rebecca unmuted the volume and

clicked on the flashing light.

'What are you doing up this late?' Susannah, bright and cheerful in a sunny yellow dress, beamed at the camera.

Rubbing her tired eyes, she shrugged. 'I fell asleep writing.'

'Not a good sign. I hope your readers won't do the same.'

Arguing that no-one else would ever read her work would only kick start her cousin's certainty that Rebecca was the next bestselling author.

'Thought I'd check in for an update on the next great romance before my dishy fiancé comes to . . .'

'Fiancé?' Rebecca shrieked.

Susannah waved her left hand at the screen and showed off a gorgeous diamond ring sparkled in the light.

'For a whole thirteen hours.'

'I need all the details.' Hopefully a plastered-on smile would fool her cousin. She didn't need any encouragement to launch into a minute-by-minute description of the whole romantic event which demanded nothing of Rebecca apart from the occasional exclamation of amazement.

Chris had excelled himself by picking Susannah up in a vintage white Rolls-Royce and whisking her off to dinner at Nathan Outlaw's famous Michelin-starred restaurant in Rock.

'I've eaten great seafood in California but it was truly out of this world.' Susannah sighed. 'Chris managed to get us a table because one of his old schoolfriends is the head bartender.'

'How did he propose?'

The question set off another dreamy sigh and a recitation of Chris's poetic plea for Susannah to become his wife, on bended knee in front of the packed restaurant.

Totally against Rebecca's usual love of privacy, she found herself deeply envious of such a public proclamation of love. She refused to dent her cousin's glow by mentioning how short a time they'd known each other or the obstacles to making a life together. Who was she to preach?

'Are you listening?' Susannah's cross tone of voice cut through Rebecca's gloom and she struggled to smile again. 'If you're at all interested I've just asked you to be my bridesmaid.'

'Of course I'm interested and I'd be thrilled!'

'Good.' Her cousin softened. 'There's no-one else I'd rather have. We're thinking October there in Nashville, because that's home to me rather than Florida. I told Mom and Dad last night and they're good with that.'

'Can you organise a full-scale wedding in only six months?'

Susannah scoffed.

'No, but we don't want anything fancy.'

'You've changed.' Rebecca laughed. 'When we were eleven you planned every detail of your imaginary wedding down to the antique white lace napkins and the tall, dark and handsome millionaire bridegroom.'

'Haven't you changed, too, since then?'

A silence stretched between them.

'Some changes don't happen by choice,' Rebecca murmured and immediately wished she'd kept quiet. 'Sorry, I don't mean to spoil your moment. It doesn't matter if you get married in a friend's back garden instead of Westminster Abbey, or if the groom is a reserved Cornish solicitor rather than a wealthy entrepreneur.' Rebecca reached out to touch her cousin's face on the screen. 'You love him and he obviously loves you. That's the only important fact.' Her throat tightened.

'Hey, don't get all sloppy on me.' Susannah gulped. 'Chris will be here in a minute and I don't need to be panda-eyed when he arrives. We're having lunch with his folks to break the good news.'

Her nose wrinkled.

'Although I'm not sure they'll think of it that way. We got on OK when we met a couple of weeks ago but I'm pretty sure they're not expecting their conservative, cautious only son to rush into marriage with a mouthy natura-lised American he hasn't known five minutes.'

'*Is anything worthwhile ever easy?*'

'You'll be fine and at the end of the day it's Chris you're marrying, not his parents. I know their opinion matters but he obviously thought this through and knows what he wants — you.'

'You're right. Look, I've got to go. Get some sleep and I'll give you a buzz again, maybe tomorrow. Perhaps you'll have some good news to share by then.'

Rebecca did the forced-smile thing again. She refused to put a dent in her cousin's joy by bemoaning her own see-saw relationship with a certain man.

With a quick wave she turned off the computer before resting her head on her folded arms and finally letting out the tears that had been stuck in her throat ever since Zac cancelled their lunch date.

She knew him well enough to read between the few terse words and realise something was very wrong.

Make or Break

This morning the lyrics fell into place which wasn't a great surprise. 'No More Chances Tonight' about summed up Zac's life.

He parked outside the ballet studio but couldn't face going in to hang around with the other waiting parents.

Last night he'd been a coward twice. First by avoiding any mention of Rebecca and not asking Harper why she'd lied to his mother. He'd rationalised it by admitting his own niggling doubts about why Rebecca hesitated to talk about her family, even after he'd opened up about his marriage.

The second cowardly act had been Zac cancelling his lunch date with Rebecca without giving a genuine explanation.

Neither sat well with him. So much for encouraging Harper to be honest.

'There you are, Daddy!' Harper raced out of the door and hurtled towards him.

'Ava's mom thought you hadn't come and was going to call you but I promised her you'd be waiting for me.'

If he didn't put Harper first no-one else would, but that didn't mean letting her get away with the sort of behaviour she pulled yesterday.

'Can I go home with Ava? They're . . .'

'No, sweetheart.'

'But — '

'No. Not today.' He stuck to his resolution. 'You've homework to finish and I need to talk you about some important things.'

Harper rolled her eyes.

Only after they'd finished their dinner, reheated leftovers from Sunday, and studied for this week's spelling test, for once without tears, did he raise the topic of Rebecca.

'You enjoyed going to the zoo on Saturday?'

'Yes.' Harper drew out her answer

and gave him a puzzled look.

'And did having Ava and Rosie come along, too, make it more fun for you?'

This time she simply nodded. His daughter wasn't stupid and no doubt guessed he was inching his way around to saying something she probably wouldn't like.

'You all seemed to get on well with Rebecca.'

'She's OK, I guess.'

Not wonderful but he persevered.

'You were kind when she talked to us about losing her brother. That must have been a real hard time for her.'

Harper shrugged.

'Did she say anything else about Harry when I wasn't around?'

'No.' The word emerged on a whisper.

Zac leaned across the kitchen table and touched her arm.

'Then where did you hear the story you told Momma Betsy? Or did you make it up?' She gave him a wide-eyed stare and Zac drove home his point.

'Why would you do that?'

'Because she's dumb and wants to take you away from me and I'm not going to let her!' Harper yelled and burst into tears.

The childish, irrational logic sucked his breath away. He wrapped his arms around her and murmured the soothing words he'd become an expert in over the last ten years. If he messed up now, Zac could forget any hope of bringing Rebecca into the tight family circle he'd created with his daughter.

'Are you too old to sit on my lap?'

She shook her head and shifted over to snuggle into him.

'We talked about Rebecca being my special friend and I thought you were OK with that? There's enough of me to go around,' he joked. But Harper didn't smile.

'Uncle Aaron and Uncle Noah were talking. They didn't know I was there.'

'What have I told you about eaves-dropping?'

'That it's wrong,' she grumbled.

'Ignoring that for a minute, what did your uncles say?'

'That Rebecca is pretty and you were lucky and wouldn't it be cool for me to have a stepmother.' Harper rattled out the words. 'But I don't want her telling me what to do and being mean!'

'Do you and your friends ever talk about things you don't know much about?'

'I guess.'

'Well, that's what your uncles were doing. If I'm thinking about getting married again I'll talk to you about it first — not them.'

'Promise?' Her earnest plea touched him.

'Pinky promise.' Zac held up his little finger and they entwined them the same as they'd done since she was a little girl. 'I need a promise from you, too.'

'I won't make up stories again.'

'I hope you won't but that's not what's bothering me most. If you're worried about anything I want you to

188

come and tell me. Between us we can sort it out.'

'You want her to be your girlfriend instead of girl friend?'

Zac struggled how to answer.

'There's not a lot of point telling me — you've got to ask her first.' With an exaggerated sigh Harper turned the tables on him. 'Even I know that.'

'Yeah, it might be best.' He cracked a smile, relieved when his daughter couldn't resist smiling back. 'Maybe she could come for dinner on Friday night?'

'Your cooking might put her off. Get Grandma to make a lasagne.'

'O ye of little faith,' Zac teased. 'Rebecca might prefer her meatloaf burned!'

'You're hopeless, Daddy. I'm going to get ready for bed. I expect hot chocolate with marshmallows when I come down.'

Her way of telling him they were OK brought a lump to his throat.

'Deal.'

★　★　★

189

If she could push Zac from her mind Rebecca totally loved her life here. She'd settled into an enjoyable routine of waking early without the aid of an alarm clock before enjoying her breakfast out on Susannah's back deck, still in her pyjamas.

She'd prop up her laptop on the table and edit yesterday's writing before taking a shower and getting dressed. Around 10 came a brisk walk around the neighbourhood before she ended up at one of the coffee shops. Then she returned to the house, made a sandwich to eat at her desk and knuckled down to work, rarely stopping until hunger and an aching back nudged her into realising how late it was.

Rebecca prodded the salmon she was cooking and decided to give it another couple of minutes. Instead of the convenience food she relied on back home she'd forced herself to cook more healthily until it had become a pleasure. She tracked down new recipes online and walked to the nearby Turnip Truck shop for supplies.

Her phone buzzed and Rebecca sneaked a glance to see Zac's number.

'Oh, hi.' Stay cool, she told herself.

Zac sighed.

'There's a lot I need to say but two things will do for now. One is that I'm an idiot and the second is will you come to dinner with me and Harper on Friday night?'

Rebecca could insist on clearing the air now but something told her to back off.

'I'd love to. Thanks for the invitation.'

'I'll pick you up at five, if that's OK?'

Zac's careful polite tone bothered her. He shouldn't need to tiptoe around her.

'Perfect. Can I bring anything? Perhaps a dessert?'

'I should say no,' he said, laughing, 'but I'm not completely dumb. That would be great. I warn you now I'm bucking my daughter's advice.'

I can believe that, Rebecca thought. I'm pretty sure she doesn't want me within a five-mile radius of you.

'She swore my cooking would put you off and told me to persuade my mother to make one of her wonderful lasagnes.' Zac hesitated a second. 'But I'm not gonna be dishonest with you, which means you get my world-famous fried chicken. I learned it from my grandmother and it's my only date-impressing recipe.'

Rebecca wondered if she dared to crack a joke, but he forestalled her.

'Yeah, I know. If it's that good why am I still single?' His warm laugh trickled down the phone. 'You'll find out on Friday, I guess.'

'I will indeed.'

'I wish . . . ' A lengthy silence hung between them.

'What is it that you wish, Zac?' she whispered.

'That I was there with you. I'd wrap you in my arms and kiss you and tell you how much you mean to me.'

'Maybe it's better you're not.' Rebecca's voice wobbled. 'We ought to do the

192

talking thing first.'

'Are you always this sensible?' Zac half-heartedly complained. 'That's usually my job.'

'You've done it for ten years so perhaps it's time for a break.'

'There's no vacation from responsibility when you've got a kid.'

'A clear warning if ever I heard one.'

'Honey.' He cleared his throat. 'If you're looking for a carefree man with no other calls on his time and energy I'm not the one for you.'

Rebecca wished they were in the same room, not simply because she craved his reassuring touch, but because the overwhelming need to see Zac's familiar face tore her apart.

'Do I seriously need to answer?'

'No, sweetie,' he groaned. 'It's me being stupid again. I'm not sure if I'm testing you or me.'

'Go now and do your dad stuff. Will you ring me tomorrow night?'

'You'd better believe it.'

They dragged out their goodnights

and Rebecca stared at the phone long after Zac hung up.

Friday was make or break time. She'd cross her fingers for 'make'.

We All Have Dreams

Zac fingered the invitation — not exactly the right word choice in the circumstances but correct vocabulary was the least of his worries.

'Daddy, I've laid the table and picked some flowers from the garden.'

As Harper raced into the kitchen, he shoved the card in his jeans' pocket to ask Rebecca's opinion later. That was if she survived his cooking and Harper's sudden attack of helpfulness. The latter shouldn't put him on edge but she'd thrown herself into the preparations for tonight with a suspicious amount of enthusiasm.

'Great. I'm heading off to pick up Rebecca in a couple of minutes.'

'Can I come?'

Zac bit back the instant refusal balanced on the tip of his tongue.

'Of course you can.' At least it would

stop her sabotaging the meal while he was out. Don't be negative, he told himself.

'Come and see.' She tugged on his hand and dragged him towards the dining-room.

'Oh, wow!' Dumbstruck, he stared around at the huge pink hearts stuck all over the walls, dangling from the light fixture and strewn over the table.

Zac peered closer and saw his and Rebecca's names entwined on the hearts, courtesy of Harper's favourite purple glitter pen. He caught her watching and fixed his smile in place.

'I can't believe you did all this.'

Harper's cheeks burned as his smart daughter picked up on the double meaning behind his words.

'Rebecca will be surprised,' he said. She'll probably want to flee!'

'*But that's your plan, isn't it?*' he added silently. A faint sliver of uncertainty flitted across her face but she didn't blink.

He considered sending Rebecca a

warning text but refused to play Harper's game. The ten-minute drive with his daughter chattering away as normal grated on Zac's patience.

When he stopped outside the house she flung open her door and jumped out. So much for snatching a few seconds alone.

'I do like a prompt man.' Rebecca laughed as she opened the door before he could ring the bell. 'Oh, Harper, it's lovely to see you again. Thanks for coming to get me.'

Zac received a fleeting impression of a rich deep blue dress skimming down over tempting curves and struggled not to stare.

'It's our pleasure.'

He gestured towards the back seat and Harper obediently got in, probably deciding she'd better not press her luck.

'Your daddy tells me cooking isn't really his thing,' Rebecca joked.

'He's not too bad but we do have the nearest pizza and Chinese restaurants on speed dial.'

Zac considered protesting but both females laughed which he chalked up as a baby step in the right direction.

'Have you tried any cooking yourself?'

'Grandma's taught me a few things.'

'That's the best way to learn. My mother was an amazing cook and now I wished I paid more attention. I've attempted a lot of new recipes recently so maybe you'd like to come over and sample my cooking one day?'

He caught his daughter's fading smile in the mirror.

'We don't have much spare time. Do we, Daddy?'

'No, but it's extremely kind of Ms Rebecca to invite us and I'm sure we could fit it in.'

'You can if you want.' Harper grunted and slumped back in the seat.

'Sorry,' Zac murmured, embarrassed by his daughter's bad manners.

'No problem.' The high colour in her cheeks betrayed Rebecca's discomfort but he let it go.

'Right, ladies, out you get.' One sight of the dining-room could send this evening completely down the tank. 'Harper, why don't you watch TV while I show Ms Rebecca the trick to my famous fried chicken?'

'I'd rather help you.' She stared him down.

'Good idea,' Rebecca agreed. 'I'm sure he needs all the help he can get.'

'I certainly do.' Zac played along.

How did other single parents date without alienating their children? One glance at Rebecca, wearing her usual kind smile and asking his daughter about her ballet classes, toughened his resolution.

'First lesson in chicken frying coming up.'

★　★　★

Harper's resentment level see-sawed all the way through the process of getting dinner ready and Rebecca couldn't help but ache for the girl. This in-between stage of life was hard enough without throwing a rival for her father's affection into the mix.

'Would you like me to lay the table?' she offered.

'There's no need. We did it earlier, didn't we, sweetheart?' Zac said and Rebecca picked up on the girl's surprise.

'Don't try to take all the credit, Daddy.' Harper glared. 'I did it by myself!'

Her voice wobbled but her focus on Rebecca never faltered.

'I'm sure you've done an awesome job.'

'She has indeed.' Zac's loving gaze rested on his daughter. 'Why don't you take Ms Rebecca into the dining-room and I'll bring the food?'

'Fine.'

A few seconds later Rebecca fought to hold back a rash of giggles.

'I can't believe you went to all this trouble.' The flush of heat on Harper's neck deepened. 'This is so intricate.'

She picked up one of the paper hearts.

'It must have taken you hours.'

'I guess,' Harper mumbled.

'Do you enjoy art at school? You're very talented.'

The girl's dark brown eyes, the mirror image of Zac's, widened. She'd expected to be told off but Rebecca suspected her father had already done that.

'It's my favourite class. I suppose I'm OK.'

'I've never been artistic but I love writing so that's my creative outlet.'

Zac came in balancing several steaming dishes of food and she sneaked him a surreptitious wink while Harper filled their water glasses. His stiff shoulders relaxed and a tiny smile twitched the corner of his mouth.

'Ms Rebecca loves my decorations.' The hint of defiance made Rebecca smile. 'She says I'm talented.'

Zac's eyes sparkled.

'You certainly are, honey bunch.'

They settled down to eat and part-way through the meal, when they were all laughing and telling stories, a flashback of her own family seated around the table one Sunday lunchtime slammed into Rebecca. For a few panicked seconds she couldn't breathe until Zac's hand slid over hers, wrapping her in his steady, warm strength.

'That was delicious. I'm so full I might burst!' She set down her knife and fork. Apart from the crispy fried chicken he'd made creamy mashed potatoes, green beans and coleslaw to go along with it and she'd happily sampled everything.

'You've no room for cake? What a lightweight,' he teased.

'If I eat cake now the words 'light' and 'weight' definitely won't apply.' Rebecca joked back at him. 'You go ahead but I'd prefer to wait until later, if that's OK?'

'Me, too, Daddy.' Harper's agreement took her by surprise. 'Have you ever seen the 'Princess Diaries' movies, Ms Rebecca? The first one is my absolute favourite. We could watch it.'

'I love them, and that sounds great if your father doesn't mind. When the film came out I was a couple of years older than Mia but I still identified with her.'

'Don't tell me you're an undercover princess, too?' Zac joked.

'I mean the part about not fitting in at school. I'd just lost my family and no-one knew how to treat me.'

Harper nodded.

'Everybody's got a mom apart from me and people are weird about it sometimes. When the news spread around school the other day about my mom . . . '

Rebecca didn't dare look at Zac. What she said now could make or break this new fragile connection with his daughter.

'It's not because they don't care, but most people haven't got a clue what to say when someone dies. One day, when it's the other way around, you'll remember how it feels and know that saying anything, no matter how awkward, is better than ignoring it. All people need is to know you care.'

She rested a hand on Harper's thin shoulder.

'Let's go and immerse ourselves in tiaras and fancy ball gowns.'

'I'll clean up dinner.' Zac's raspy voice betrayed his own emotions.

'We can help first.'

'No, it's OK. Trust me,' he insisted. 'Harper knows my tolerance for princess movies is pretty low.'

'Men!'

'Shoo.' Zac waved them away and Harper immediately raced off. Before Rebecca could leave he pulled her close for a quick kiss. 'You're amazing.'

'It's no hardship. I honestly love the film.'

Zac's eyes darkened.

'That's not all I meant.'

'I know.'

'Later.'

With another playful kiss he let go and began to pick up the dirty dishes.

Joining Harper on the sofa she followed the girl's lead and didn't attempt to restart their previous conversation. They were soon immersed and Rebecca could have cried as the girl rested against her shoulder.

When Zac finished kitchen duties he joined them and stretched out in a well-worn brown leather recliner, resting his hands behind his head and closing his eyes.

'Daddy, you'll miss the ball scene if you don't wake up.'

'Yes, Zac, you'll miss the best part,' Rebecca chimed in. 'This is where we imagine ourselves wearing an extravagant ball gown with a glittering tiara and taking on the responsibility of becoming a princess and heir to the throne of Genovia.'

He shook his head at them both.

'You're as bad as she is.' Zac nodded at his daughter. 'I wouldn't have thought it of a sensible grown woman.'

'We all have dreams,' she said softly. 'Don't you ever picture yourself winning a Grammy?'

'Daddy's got one of those. It's in the upstairs bathroom,' Harper declared and Rebecca burst out laughing as Zac turned a deep, hot shade of red.

'Seriously?'

'Yeah.' He shrugged. 'Lots of people around here have them.'

'You don't accept praise well, do you?'

'And you do?' Zac tossed back at her.

'We'll continue this later.'

'I thought we might,' he conceded with a heavy sigh. 'Time for dessert, I think, and then it's a certain young lady's bedtime.'

'But it's Friday and I always . . . ' Harper's protest faded away under her father's steady gaze. 'Fine.'

Words of Love

Zac pulled out the crumpled card and passed it across to Rebecca.

'I know we've other things to talk about, but tell me what you think of this.'

She read it through several times without making any comment.

'You're wondering whether to take Harper.'

'Yeah.'

Her deep blue eyes settled on him and Zac couldn't help wishing for one evening alone with Rebecca minus any problems. Surely it wasn't too much to ask?

'I know it's an overrated word but this would allow her a degree of closure. Sadly she'll never know her mother but at least this gives her the chance to say goodbye.'

It had surprised him to receive the

invitation from Louisa's attorney to a small memorial service being held in a week's time at her old church in Franklin.

'I'm surprised they're having it here. She's no family left that I'm aware of and she'd lived in Los Angeles for the past decade. I'd have thought all her friends were there.'

Rebecca gave a small shrug.

'Is this where you got married?'

Zac nodded through a blur of tears.

'I don't know what's wrong with me. I've barely thought about her for ten years and now . . .'

'You're grieving.' Her voice soothed him. 'It takes us all in different ways.'

Maybe this wasn't the right moment but sometimes moments needed to be made. Zac shifted to sit next to her on the sofa and took hold of her hands. They'd abandoned their plan to go out on the porch when it had started to rain.

'You've helped Harper by being so open. Are you ready to share with me exactly what happened to your family?'

He instantly wondered if he'd come across as accusatory.

'I don't . . . '

'It's all right. I've wanted to tell you for weeks.' Rebecca straightened up. 'There's some truth in Harper's story.'

'How the heck do you know about that?'

'She told me.' A small flicker of amusement brightened her sombre eyes. 'Actually, I'd call it more of a confession made during a slow part in the film earlier.'

'Wow, I'm surprised and . . . impressed.'

'You should be. She's one brave girl.'

Zac picked up on a slight reprimand lurking in her words.

'Braver than her father?'

'I wouldn't go that far.'

'But?'

'You won't push me into condemning you. I'm no better.'

He could come up with a million ways to describe how much better a person she was but kept his mouth shut and waited.

'I was seventeen and, like I said to Harper, I desperately wanted to fit in at school. I begged to go on a weekend trip to London.' Rebecca grimaced. 'When I was at a West End theatre watching 'The Lion King' my family was . . . ' Her breath caught on a sob. 'My dad told my mum he'd given up smoking but one day I caught him sneaking one after she'd gone to bed.'

'That doesn't make you guilty.'

'I should have told her!' Rebecca cried. 'Dad swore he'd stop and pleaded with me not to say anything. That evening he dropped a cigarette butt in the chair and it smouldered after they went to bed. By the time a neighbour out walking his dog spotted the fire and called the fire brigade it was too late.'

'You can't blame yourself.'

'Why not? Wouldn't you?' she pressed. Zac couldn't lie.

'Yep, I'm afraid I would.' He struggled for words. 'Doesn't make it right, though. My family have been going on at me for years to date again. They insist it's not

210

good to revolve my life around Harper, for both our sakes.' His self-deprecating shrug returned a touch of humour to Rebecca's grim features. 'I guess you're no better at listening than me.'

'Maybe that's why we're drawn to each other. Two damaged souls.' She struggled to smile.

'What did you do . . . afterwards?'

'The house wasn't badly damaged and I insisted on staying. I threw a fit when they told me I couldn't live there alone because I was under eighteen.' Rebecca's face tightened. 'I talked a distant cousin into officially 'living' with me for a few months to satisfy social services.'

'But she didn't?'

'She sort of did. Enough to placate the nosy neighbours, and she took care of the money side of things.' Her chin took on a defiant tilt. 'On my eighteenth birthday I took control and I've never relied on anyone since then.'

'Relying on and sharing with are two different things in my book,' Zac ventured. 'Are you good with the idea of sharing?'

Rebecca's heart raced.

'What precisely are you asking?'

'I'm not sure . . . yet.' A lazy smile made its way across his face and he stroked her cheek, heating her skin with the tip of his finger. 'I'm not Susannah's impetuous fiancé. That's not me. There are too many pieces to the equation from where I'm sitting.'

'I'm good at maths.'

'I'm lousy,' he admitted. 'Perhaps I should marry you so you could help Harper with her homework.' The colour leached from Zac's face. 'I didn't mean to . . .'

'Propose?' Rebecca grinned. 'What a shame. I picked the ring out last week and I've got my eye on a stunning designer wedding dress.'

'Your wicked sense of humour will come back around and bite you on the tail one day,' he groused.

'You mean you weren't serious?' Her attempt to keep a straight face failed when he made a grab for her waist and wrestled her back on the sofa to tickle her until Rebecca begged for mercy. The moment did an abrupt U-turn as their eyes met and the world, their world, tilted off its axis.

'I'm totally serious.' Zac whispered against her neck. 'About loving you.'

'I love you, too.'

'Thank heavens for that.' He pushed his hands up through her hair and drew her close for a long, mind-blowing kiss before easing away with a frustrated sigh. 'You sure do tempt me to forget any notion of common sense.'

Rebecca smiled.

'If it's any help it's the same for me.'

Zac pulled her into his arms, snuggling into the corner of the sofa.

'Tell me about the book you're writing.'

'My book?'

'Humour me.' He gave a wry grin.

'Might stop me saying something reckless.'

'Deep down we aren't a reckless

couple, are we?'

'Is that good or bad?'

'I'm not sure.' Rebecca shrugged. 'I suspect accepting Susannah's offer used up my recklessness quota for the year.'

Zac's hand slid down to cup her chin.

'So for argument's sake, if I came up with a reckless idea on January the first next year, you might go for it?'

'It's a distinct possibility.'

Pure unadulterated joy bubbled up through her and exploded into a kiss he didn't see coming but responded to with enthusiasm.

'You asked about my book.' Her trembling voice brought out another of Zac's tempting smiles.

'I sure did.'

Haltingly she began to explain the premise behind 'A Touch More Than Friendly' and her nervousness disappeared.

'The inspiration for my hero came from you, but he's not you, I promise. For a start he's . . . '

'Not as good looking?'

214

'Searching for compliments again, Quinn?'

'Hey, I'm good with the idea of inspiring anyone — especially you. Anyway, we're even on this. You're the reason behind my new song, but it's not our story.'

'I'd love to hear it.'

'My guitar's in the other room.' He stood up from the sofa and gave her a searching look. 'The title is 'No More Chances Tonight'. That's the main reason I hope it's not our story.'

A strange attack of nerves clutched at Rebecca as Zac returned and perched on a stool by the breakfast bar. If she was ever published her work would be out there for anyone to read, and Zac wrote music for people to hear, but being the first for each other this way seemed significant.

'Here goes.' Zac bent over the guitar and strummed a haunting melody:

'He'd get no more chances tonight,
He knew when she walked out the door instead of into his arms,

When she spoke at him instead of to him,

But the saddest thing,

The one he'd remember for ever,

Was her deep blue eyes reflecting his heartbreak right back at him;

There'd be no more chances tonight to put things right.'

His broad hands stilled the strings and Rebecca struggled to rein in her emotions.

'You gonna give me a chance?' The growl in his voice got to her so she could only nod and move closer to him.

'Always.' She rested her head against his shoulder. 'That was so beautiful but you're right — it's not us.'

'When I wrote it I was afraid it might be,' Zac confessed. 'I thought I'd blown things with you before we even got started.'

Rebecca blushed.

'The feeling was mutual.' She tried to lighten things. 'I'd say you've got another Grammy winner on your hands there.'

'You're never going to let me forget that, are you?'

'Why should I? It's awesome!'

Zac set down the guitar and wrapped his arms around her.

'No. This is awesome. That was simply a hit song.'

A Chance to Say Goodbye

He'd asked everyone's opinion except the one person who really mattered, and the overwhelming verdict came down in favour of letting Harper make up her own mind.

'What do you think? If you want to go to the memorial service Grandma, Pappy and Aunt Nikki are happy to come with us.'

Harper frowned.

'They can if they like but I want Ms Rebecca, too.'

'OK.' Zac hid his surprise. 'We can ask.'

'She'll say yes.'

His daughter's confidence warmed Zac.

'I'll call her now if you give me the phone.' Harper stuck out her hand and waited for him to hand it over. 'She's my friend, too. I'll ask her.'

'Hi, it's Harper.' The trace of a wobble in her voice as she explained why she was calling pained Zac but he didn't interrupt.

'Thanks. That's cool. See you Saturday.'

She thrust the phone at him.

'She wants to talk to you. I'm going to get my homework done.'

Before he could ask any questions Harper disappeared upstairs.

'You have an amazing daughter.'

'She sure is.' Zac cleared his throat. 'I hope you don't mind too much?'

'Mind? Are you crazy?' Rebecca laughed. 'I'm blown away by her wanting me there. I hope it won't upset the rest of your family? I don't want to intrude.'

He quickly reassured her that anything or anybody who could make the difficult experience easier would be welcomed with open arms.

'You'll help me, too.'

'I hope so.' Zac sensed her hesitate.

'Harper insists she needs something

new to wear on Saturday. If choosing a special outfit makes this a bit easier on her that's all the justification we need. I said we'd take her shopping.'

'You did?'

'Yes, is that a problem?'

'No, ma'am.' He agreed to pick Rebecca up next day to go to the mall — his least favourite place on the planet.

★　★　★

Rebecca's hands froze at the keyboard. The scratching noise grew louder and she glanced across to see the front door knob turning from side to side. She fumbled in the piles of papers sprawled over the kitchen table in a fruitless search for the phone and a scream lodged in her throat as the door bounced open against the wall.

'Surprise!' Susannah threw several bags down on the floor and flung open her arms, posing like a movie star on the red carpet.

'For heaven's sake, you almost gave me a heart attack! What are you doing here?'

'It's my house, in case you'd forgotten.'

'You didn't think to let me know you were coming?'

'I thought it'd be a neat surprise.'

'Oh, it's a surprise, all right.' Rebecca wasn't quite ready to forgive, considering her hands still shook and her heart bounced against her chest. She glanced behind Susannah. 'Is Chris with you?'

'No.' Her face settled into grim lines.

'Just no?'

Susannah shrugged.

'We sort of split up. I'm not sure.'

Surely they were either engaged or not? Rebecca couldn't see any middle ground.

'Do you want to talk about it?'

'Not really.' Susannah grimaced. 'I'm absolutely shattered. That journey's a killer. Fix me a cup of tea and then I'll be off to bed.'

'I'll put the kettle on. It'll only take

me a few minutes to change the sheets.'

'Don't worry about it — I'll take the guest room.'

Susannah slumped on the sofa and kicked off her shoes.

'How's the bestseller coming on?'

'Because you're tired I won't argue the point. My writing's going well.'

'And your love life?'

Rebecca blushed.

'Not bad.'

Susannah's eyes gleamed.

'OMG, Zac's proposed, hasn't he? You sneaky thing.'

'No. Well, not exactly.'

Cautiously she started to explain everything and by the end her cousin stared at her in open admiration.

'Wow. You've really tossed your hat in the ring. I never saw you as potential stepmother material but obviously you've changed.'

Rebecca gave a slight shrug.

'Generally speaking I wouldn't either but Harper . . . that's different.'

She decided to take a chance and

press Susannah a little more.

'Did Chris's parents spoil things between you? They've always been a close-knit family and I get the impression he helps them out a lot these days.'

Her cousin's smile faded.

'I never had any intention of taking him away but that's how they saw things working out.'

'Didn't he stand up for you?'

Susannah lay back on the cushions with her eyes closed.

'Chris tried to defend me but it was . . . half-hearted. At least in my opinion.'

'So you argued. That's why you're here and he's in Cornwall.'

Rebecca's neat summing up made Susannah sigh and drag herself back up to sitting.

'Yeah, that's about it. I'm off to bed. You can continue your agony aunt role in the morning — or should that be agony cousin?'

'I will do.'

On a whim she wrapped her arms

around her lovelorn cousin.

'I hate seeing you so miserable.'

'Hey, if anyone knows about miserable it's you.' Susannah tried to smile. 'I'm glad I came now.'

'Distance often helps.'

'It seems to be working for you.'

Rebecca nodded.

'It certainly does, thanks to you. Now it's repayment time.'

She determined to put the love back in her cousin's eyes where it belonged.

All's Well . . .

Rebecca wriggled further under the bedcovers to blot out the sound of Susannah and Chris yelling at each other.

Correction — her cousin hadn't stopped screaming at the top of her voice while Chris patiently answered her back.

An hour ago he had turned up on the doorstep, pale and red-eyed with exhaustion but determined to whisk Susannah back to Cornwall.

Loud footsteps thundered up the stairs.

'I've never met such an impossible man.' Susannah burst into the bedroom. 'I told him I wanted time to think, so why did he follow me on the next flight?'

'Because he loves you.' Rebecca stated the obvious and her cousin burst into tears. 'Chris knew if he didn't come you'd never forgive him.'

'You think I should apologise and talk to him quietly, don't you?'

'It's none of my business.'

'You're going to make me spell it out, aren't you?' Susannah groused. 'I'm asking for advice. Are you happy now?'

'Absolutely.' Rebecca grinned. 'I do think that's the only adult way to sort out the situation. And please, really listen to Chris instead of assuming what you think he says.'

Rebecca leaned forward.

'Zac and I are still working on that very same thing. It's not easy. You're a take-charge sort of woman and although Chris may be quiet he's not a pushover.'

'I guess you're right.'

'I'll stay out of the way and wait to hear the good news.' Rebecca wagged her finger. 'Don't take too long because I'm starving and dying for a cup of tea.'

'I'll go and grovel. I won't be long.'

She breezed out and left Rebecca pondering on the drastic change in both of their lives over two short months. Who would have thought a casual decision to swap houses could have such an impact?

★ ★ ★

'Wake up, sleepyhead. We've got news.'

Rebecca struggled to open her eyes.

'Here you go. Tea and toast.'

Rebecca glanced over Susannah's shoulder to see Chris lurking in the doorway wearing a sheepish expression.

'So are you two, um . . . '

'Engaged again? We certainly are.' He beamed. 'Aren't we, sweetheart? As Shakespeare said 'All's well that ends well'.' Chris grabbed his fiancée and waved around her left hand to show off the newly reinstated ring. 'There's a change of wedding plans, though.'

'We're getting married in Cornwall. Chris's parents aren't well enough to travel, but mine are, so this way they can all be there for us.' Susannah's gaze softened as it rested on him. 'We want to make Cornwall our permanent base anyway, so it makes sense.'

'That's wonderful. I couldn't be happier.'

'Oh, you certainly will be when Mr Zac Quinn puts a ring on your finger.'

Rebecca sighed.

'Don't push us. We'll get there when the time's right. Off you go while I finish breakfast.' She shooed them out, shoving away an unwanted niggle of jealousy.

★ ★ ★

Zac struggled to say something.

'Don't you like it, Daddy?' Harper's worried voice trickled into his brain and he saw Rebecca frowning in the background.

'Honey, I love it. You look lovely. Grown up and not my little girl any more.'

The adorable black and white flowery dress, full skirted and with a black satin belt, fell just above the knee.

'It came with a short cardigan Harper can pop on in the church and we also bought cute black velvet flat shoes to wear with it.'

Zac knew he was being ridiculous but that didn't make it any easier.

'Ms Rebecca's offered to help with my hair on Saturday.' Harper beamed. 'She's been practising how to do braids.'

He cleared his throat.

'That's really kind. Thanks.'

'You're welcome.'

For once Zac wished she couldn't read him quite as well.

'You'd better get changed, poppet. We need to leave in a few minutes or you'll be late for Girl Scouts.'

When he was back at the house with Rebecca everything inside him crumbled.

'If I didn't have to drive I'd sink a large whisky right now.'

'I'm sorry, Zac, but you'll have to get over this.' Rebecca held up one hand. 'And don't say I can't understand because I'm not a parent. The Christmas I turned twelve my mum bought me a red dress and Dad reacted the exact same way as you.

'Actually he was worse, because he didn't hide it as well and yelled at my mum, ordering her to take the dress back to the shop.' She smiled. 'Mum stood up for me and in the end he caved. But it spoiled the dress for me and dented my confidence.'

'The last thing I want is to do that.'

'Did she remind you of Louisa?' Rebecca's soft question ripped him apart and Zac could only nod. 'I thought so. You can't blame Harper for that.'

'I'm not blaming her!' His anguish erupted. 'But the last thing I want is her to turn out the same way. Louisa saw her looks as the most important thing in the world.' Zac grabbed Rebecca. 'Everything you say is logical, but I'm still scared.'

'Listen to yourself. This isn't who you are, Zac, and it's not who Harper is, either. You're a wonderful father and you've brought Harper up well. Plus she's surrounded by a loving family.' Tears glistened in her eyes. 'That is such a gift.'

'I know,' he muttered.

'It'll get harder still before it gets easier again,' Rebecca warned. 'That's the nature of teenagers. I'm sure you gave your parents a hard time.'

He cracked a smile.

'Yeah, I wasn't always the perfect man you see today.'

'You do surprise me.' The quick, dry response made him laugh.

'You're a wonderful woman.'

'Yes, well, you keep thinking that and we'll be fine.' Rebecca pressed a hard kiss on his mouth. 'Change of subject. You've got to hear all about Susannah and her on again, off again engagement.'

By the time they were laughing together about the vagaries of love he'd pushed his worries away.

'When's the wedding?'

'They were aiming for October but I don't think they're going to wait that long. Thankfully Chris knows all the legal ins and outs, so that shouldn't be a problem. I heard them mention July as a possibility.'

A flutter of panic shot through Zac.

'Don't go off the deep end,' she warned. 'I'm not talking about us, am I?'

'No.'

'When are you going to really trust me?' The sadness in her eyes tugged at him. 'We agreed to be honest and that's what I'm doing. If you think I'm in a hurry to rush down the aisle you couldn't be more wrong.'

Why didn't that make him happy, either? Heavens, he was a contrary man.

'I've got about a month left here. Please don't spoil it.'

Zac clearly heard her silent question about what would happen next. Instead of answering, he kissed her.

When the Time is Right

Zac had tried to prepare Harper but didn't do such a good job on himself. The sight of a blown-up picture of Louisa on an easel at the front of the church just about floored him.

Her blonde hair tousled by the wind, she was running barefoot on a sandy beach.

'I wish I had Mommy's hair,' Harper complained.

He pulled himself together.

'Instead of my unruly mop?'

'You've got her eyes.' Rebecca pointed to the photograph. 'And look at the shape of her mouth. Yours is the same.'

Harper's wide smile eased a hole in Zac's sadness. He'd scanned the church when they arrived and spotted a group in one corner who must be Louisa's Hollywood friends, judging by their glossy appearance and high-pitched chatter.

His own family filled up one row and a few locals sat together at the back.

'Mr Quinn?' A short man stuck out his hand. 'Randy Fallon, Ms Hardy's attorney. I wondered if you might be willing to say a few words at the conclusion?'

'Me?'

'None of her family is in attendance. Ms Hardy's cousins couldn't make it from Colorado.' Fallon's sour expression made his disapproval clear.

'Why did she want the service held here?' Zac asked.

'Happy memories?'

'I wouldn't have thought so. Louisa couldn't wait to get away.'

'We don't always make the wisest choices when we're young. I suspect she came to realise that.'

Zac glanced at his daughter, now happily chattering away to Nikki and Rebecca. At least his seemingly unwise choice had also brought him the greatest joy.

'Louisa wrote this when she was ill.'

Fallon pulled out a letter from his jacket pocket. 'It's for your daughter.'

'For Harper?'

'Louisa's instructions were for you to give it to her when you decide the time is right.'

Zac fingered the long white envelope.

'We also need to talk about her will. Are you free later today?'

'I suppose so.'

Louisa ran through money like a waterfall when they were married so he didn't imagine there would be much left.

'So you'll speak?'

Zac was haunted by Nikki's words:

'Louisa knew you'd always be there, didn't she?'

He'd be there for her one last time.

★   ★   ★

Rebecca slipped her hand into Zac's.

'Are you all right?'

'I will be when it's over.'

The service started and it didn't

seem long until the preacher called on anyone who wanted to speak. She'd done her best to calm Zac down after Louisa's lawyer talked him into taking part, and encouraged him to focus on Harper.

She smoothed Zac's jacket collar where it had turned up at the edge. Everything about him was restrained today, from the charcoal grey suit, crisp white shirt and sombre black tie to his freshly trimmed hair. Rebecca whispered Harper's name and the shadow of a smile brightened his dark eyes.

As he made his way up she unconsciously put her arm around Harper. She'd wondered if it might hurt to hear him speak about the woman he'd once loved and who'd given birth to his precious daughter, but Zac's simple eloquence only deepened her own love for him.

Harper's quiet sobs broke through her reverie and Rebecca concentrated on comforting the young girl until Zac returned to join them as the service finished.

'Why don't you all come back with

us?' Seth clapped his youngest son's shoulder.

'If it's all the same to you, Dad, we'll go on home. It's been a rough day and Louisa's attorney wants a word with me.'

The three of them headed back outside and Rebecca blinked her eyes against the blast of spring sunshine.

'Would you prefer . . . ?'

'No. You're coming with us.' Zac tightened his grasp on her hand.

'How did you know what I was going to say?'

'Because you're polite and always try to do the 'right' thing.' He brushed a kiss on her mouth. 'This is the right thing.'

'We've got chocolate ice-cream and strawberry cake,' Harper piped up.

'Oh well, that seals the deal.'

'I'm not enough?' Zac laughingly protested. 'Offer the woman cake and ice-cream and she's falling over herself to get in the car.'

Harper rolled her eyes.

'Silly Daddy.'

A lump of emotion stuck in Rebecca's throat.

'He certainly is.'

The three of them held hands and hurried down the street to the car park. From the outside they resembled a 'normal' family and Rebecca wondered what the chances were of that ever coming true?

★ ★ ★

Zac struggled to comprehend as Randy Fallon explained the details of Louisa's will for the third time. Thank heavens he'd left Harper and Rebecca watching another of their beloved 'Princess Diaries' films.

'Louisa didn't become a household name but she worked steadily over the years and lived very carefully.'

Zac had never connected the words 'steady' and 'careful' with Louisa but he kept that to himself.

'So what you're telling me is that

there's a one-million dollar trust fund set up for Harper's education and future which needs to be administered by me, with your supervision, until she turns twenty-five?'

'Precisely,' Fallon agreed. 'My suggestion, and naturally it's up to you, is to say nothing about it for now. When you start to discuss college plans you can inform Harper that her mother left enough money to cover the cost of wherever she wants to go, and leave it at that.

'Her eighteenth birthday might be a good time to explain the full extent of her mother's legacy.'

The lawyer hesitated.

'You might care to know that Ms Hardy always kept up with what you both were doing.'

'I don't get it!' Zac couldn't hide his dismay. 'Louisa wanted nothing to do with us after she left. She could have had a relationship with Harper, with visitation and everything. I don't understand why she'd sneak around online rather than play a proper part in her daughter's life.'

'People are complicated. Perhaps she didn't feel entitled to anything after leaving you both.'

'If it's true, that's sad.'

'Yes, it is.' Fallon picked up his papers. 'Obviously I'll stay in touch and let me know if there's anything I can do. Please don't bother to see me out.'

With a sigh, Zac went to join the women who had stuck by him today.

'How are my favourite girls?' He flopped down between them on the sofa.

'Shush, Daddy, this is the best part,' Harper remonstrated.

Zac put his arm around Rebecca and whispered in her ear.

'Later I'll tell you about an idea I've had and you can tell me what you think.'

He got a quizzical look in response.

'You'll have to wait. Patience is a virtue.'

★　★　★

Surprising women wasn't easy but judging by Rebecca's shocked expression he'd succeeded.

'It will mean we'd only have to survive a month or so apart. Do you think Susannah and Chris will mind us inviting ourselves?'

'I'm sure they won't.' She flung her arms around his neck. 'Oh, Zac, I've been imagining all sorts of things you could be planning to say but none involved you and Harper coming to Cornwall.'

He'd picked up on the wistfulness in her voice when she had talked about Susannah's wedding plans.

They'd avoided discussing what they'd do when Rebecca's time in Nashville came to an end, neither ready to challenge the other.

Zac looked on this trip as a halfway step and knew for all of their sakes he couldn't afford to mess this up.

'I can afford to miss a couple weeks of work but not much more.' He held her hand up against his thumping heart. 'Maybe you'll consider coming back with us?'

'I'll give it some thought.'

Rebecca's eyes sparkled and Zac pulled her to him. They could discuss the details later. This time was for them.

Reckless Proposal

Rebecca staggered under the weight of Harper's hug. She smiled over the girl's shoulder at Zac, loaded down with bags and flashing his familiar grin.

'It was absolute coolest thing ever. I had my own TV and they brought food around on tiny trays. This really cute boy sat by me and OMG his accent was like yours.'

'Are you hungry? We've got time for breakfast before our train.' Rebecca pointed to a nearby café.

'I'm starved.'

'Me, too.' Zac spoke up. 'Run on over and find us a table, Harper, and we'll bring the luggage.'

Before Rebecca could follow she found herself thoroughly kissed. She ran her fingers through Zac's tousled hair and sighed happily.

'Heck, woman, you're messing it up.'

'Right.' She dragged out the word and laughed. 'Come on, we'd better go.'

'Feed me and I'm all yours.'

Rebecca blushed.

'For a start I'll introduce you to bacon butties and proper tea. That'll do for now.' It had been a long month apart. 'It's going to be fun seeing everything through Harper's eyes.'

She hadn't travelled outside the States before and the train ride would be her first.

'It always is. Children stop you taking so much for granted.'

Taking anything for granted wasn't in her nature these days but Rebecca held back on saying that out loud.

Five hours later they arrived at the house with a tired, cranky girl on their hands because she'd refused to take a nap and miss any part of the journey.

'There you are.' Susannah opened the door before they even walked up the narrow path. 'Welcome to Cornwall, y'all.'

'How's the bride-to-be?' Zac leaned

in to kiss her cheek.

'Awesome. Everything's on track. Of course, it helps I'm not moving far.' She pointed to an adjacent house. 'That's Chris's place.'

Rebecca eyed Zac and her nervousness returned.

'If you follow me upstairs I'll show you your rooms.'

With her parents' room redecorated and ready for Zac, Rebecca had finally sorted through Harry's room for Harper to use.

'Susannah's room is across the hall and I'm down at the other end by the bathroom.' She touched Harper's arm. 'Food or sleep?'

'Sleep.'

'Wise choice.'

With her cousin nowhere in sight Rebecca offered Zac the same choices or a kiss.

'Definitely a kiss first with the right to take you up on your other offers later.'

Zac wasn't sure what he'd expected but as the days flew by he felt increasingly out of sync with Rebecca. Being here in the house dimmed her usual sparkle, as though the memories weighed her down, although things between them eased when they were out exploring.

Tonight he was determined to break down her barriers. With only two days before the wedding, Susannah was next door with Chris working on all of the last-minute details and Harper was already in bed, exhausted after a fascinating day at the Eden Project.

Zac fetched a bottle of wine and two glasses from the kitchen.

'Stop tidying up and come sit with me.'

'But I've got things I should . . . '

'Leave them. Please.' His heart skipped a beat until Rebecca put down the duster in her hand and joined him on the sofa. Zac poured the wine and passed her a glass. 'Rebecca, you know

246

I love you and I . . . hope you still love me.'

'Of course I do,' she protested. 'What are you getting at?'

Zac plunged on.

'We'd agreed to be honest with each other. If I've done something wrong or you've changed your mind about us, I need you to tell me.'

Rebecca's eyes filled with tears and her hands shook as she set the glass down on the coffee table.

'Oh, Zac, I love you more than ever.'

'Then I don't get it.'

'In Nashville us, my writing, a radical change in my life all seemed possible. But now I'm back here . . . ' Her helpless shrug broke his heart.

'You won't want to hear my theory but I'm pretty sure this house doesn't help.' He touched her forehead. 'Your family. They're up here all the time, aren't they?'

'Yes,' she whispered.

'You're convinced you don't have the right to be happy because you should have been here and prevented the fire.'

Zac gently took her hands in his.

'There's no guarantee you could have saved them, and if you'd died, too, where would I be now? What about Harper and all the other friends and people whose lives you've touched over the last sixteen years? Would your parents and Harry want you to keep on beating yourself up this way?'

'No. They wouldn't!' The strangled words emerged on a sob and she cried in his arms until there were no tears left.

'Better?'

'Yes, heaps.' Rebecca gazed up at him. 'You're a truly wonderful man.'

'But?'

'Are you sure you want an emotional mess for your . . . whatever?' A deep blush warmed her skin.

'I'm not exactly plain and straightforward myself.'

'Is that a yes or a no?'

Zac caught his breath.

'Would you care to be more specific?

A 'whatever' might be different in Cornwall. I don't want to get lost in transatlantic translation.'

'Isn't wanting to marry someone and spend your life with them the same in any language?' Rebecca protested.

'Are you proposing to me?' He couldn't hide his incredulity and she slapped a hand across her mouth.

'If it was a proposal the answer is yes.'

'Are you serious?'

'I am if you are.' Zac couldn't speak any plainer. 'I fell more than a little in love with you the moment you opened the door to me and were cross because I wasn't a woman.' He cocked his head to one side. 'I'm pretty sure you've got over that by now.'

'Yes. I much prefer you all man.' Her frown blossomed into a wide smile. 'Does that mean we're engaged?'

'Looks like it, if that's OK with you?' Not the world's most romantic declaration but she didn't seem concerned and he certainly wasn't.

'Perfect.'

'Now who's being reckless?' Zac teased. 'I'm guessing we've given up on the whole waiting until the first of January plan?'

'Yes. I've decided reckless is my new favourite thing . . . next to you, of course.'

'Heavens, I love that man.' Susannah burst into the room grinning widely. 'Saturday can't come soon . . . what's up with you pair?'

'What do you mean?' Rebecca asked, struggling to keep a straight face. 'Well, let's just say I'd be waving my left hand around right now if I hadn't put Zac on the spot and caught him unprepared.'

Zac watched the wheels turn in Susannah's head.

'Yep, you've got it right. She's going to make an honest man of me.'

'You proposed to him?' Susannah shrieked. 'OMG! You sly thing.'

'I didn't know I was going to.' Rebecca's blush deepened.

'She beat me to it, that's all,' Zac

insisted. 'Hey, this is the twenty-first century. It's all good.'

'When's the wedding? If I'm not your matron of honour I'll never speak to you again. Where will you live? What does Harper . . . '

'Slow down, for goodness sake!' Rebecca pleaded. 'We've only been engaged,' she checked her watch, 'a grand total of about five minutes.'

'You're engaged?' Harper stood at the bottom of the stairs rubbing the tiredness from her eyes. 'What's going on? I woke up and you were all talking so loud I couldn't get back to sleep.

'You promised you'd ask me first if you wanted to get married again, Daddy. I hate you!' she yelled.

Zac jumped up and blocked her escape route before she could run away.

'Sweetheart, I . . . '

'It's my fault, Harper,' Rebecca declared. 'Don't blame your father. I didn't think.'

Zac struggled to break through his daughter's understandable anger.

'She proposed to me and we were coming to wake you up when Ms Susannah delayed us.'

'There are all sorts of things we need to talk to you about,' Rebecca explained. 'For a start, I'll need a bridesmaid. How do you feel about wearing a princess dress?'

'It depends on the colour.'

'What's your favourite?'

'Red,' Harper declared with no hesitation.

'How lucky are we? That's the perfect choice for a Christmas wedding!'

'Christmas?' Zac half-choked.

'Why not? Harper will have time off school for the holidays and I'll need her help.'

Boy, how he loved this woman. The transformation in his daughter was night and day as she nodded solemnly at Rebecca.

'Are we forgiven?' His tentative question earned him a stern glare.

'I suppose so but don't do it again.'

He drew a finger across his throat.

'I promise.'

Zac gathered his favourite women in his arms for a group hug. He happily included Susannah because without her zany house-swapping idea they wouldn't be here.

In their own different ways they'd all experienced the fragility of love and its incredible strength. They'd celebrate on Saturday as Susannah and Chris made their vows, and again in December, so he'd been reliably informed, on their own special day.

Together For Ever

On the morning of Christmas Eve three monogrammed stockings hung from the stone mantel and piles of wrapped presents nestled under the beautifully decorated tree.

A fragrant aroma of fresh pine suffused the room and combined with the sparkling white lights to create an image of the perfect Christmas — except for the folding metal chairs set up anywhere they could be fitted in.

It had been Rebecca's suggestion to hold the wedding at Zac's home and only invite their immediate families, which meant 20 guests would be crammed into his living-room.

'The ceremony will only last about a quarter of an hour and then Zac's mom and all the Quinn women have a simple buffet lunch organised,' she told Susannah. 'I hope everything goes as well as it did on your big day.'

Susannah grinned.

'We ought to go and get dressed before your eager groom catches us out.'

'Becks, see my nails!' Harper raced into the room waving her hands complete with glittery scarlet polish. 'They match my dress. Aunt Nikki did them for me.'

It startled Rebecca the first time she used Harry's old nickname but when Zac asked if it bothered her she said it was good to hear it again.

'They're gorgeous.'

'She could do yours, too.'

'Thanks for the offer but I'll stick to my pale pink.' Rebecca grinned. 'I don't want to outshine my bridesmaid.'

Harper chuckled.

'Don't be silly. You've got the white dress, tiara and veil. It's no contest.'

'Absolutely no contest,' Susannah agreed. 'Come on, ladies, let's go get beautiful.'

An hour later they were done.

'I think we'll do.' Rebecca announced.

She wasn't vain but her glamorous reflection took her by surprise. The sophisticated upswept hairstyle and elegant make-up, both courtesy of Susannah, should satisfy her new family.

Family. Early this morning she had shed a few tears after allowing her parents and Harry into her mind but now she only felt wistful. She'd gain a new family today and was ready for the challenge.

'Don't you look grown up!' She twirled Harper around and the light caught the sprinkling of sequins scattered over her rich red velvet, ballerina-style dress.

'What about me?' Susannah mock-complained, parading around the room in her pale gold sheath dress.

'Yep, you look grown up, too.'

'Thanks. At least I think so. By the way, did you hear back from your agent yet?'

'Yes. She liked the first edits but there's still a long way to go.'

Thanks to Zac's urging she'd sent

her manuscript to several agents and had been amazed when one offered to represent her.

'Much better than the building society, isn't it?'

'No competition.' Everything was better now. 'Did I ever thank you?'

'Don't start again.' Susannah's raised hand shut Rebecca up. 'We've been through this a million times.'

She clapped her hands.

'I'm going to check how close things are downstairs to being ready and then I'll be back.'

★ ★ ★

Zac retreated outside on the deck to sneak a few minutes on his own. In the last nine months he and Rebecca had been through a lot, but he wouldn't change a single thing.

His reconnection with Andy had kicked his music career back into gear. Last week Rebecca was in the audience when he performed with the Time

Jumpers, standing in for one of the regulars.

He'd no interest in being a big star with the constant demands and long tours away from home but being able to make a solid living at his music would suit him fine.

'Are you ready, son?'

He smiled around at his father.

'Yeah. I've been ready a long time for this one. You ready to be my best man again? Let's do this.'

★　★　★

Zac fought to keep breathing as Rebecca floated towards him on her uncle's arm, a vision in sparkling white.

When she reached his side Zac saw through her sheer veil his own overwhelming emotion mirrored back in Rebecca's deep blue eyes. They focused their gaze on each other and spoke their vows without a hitch.

'You may kiss your bride.'

Zac's hands trembled as he lifted the

veil and smoothed it back over her gleaming hair. Later on he'd do it properly but for now he contented himself with pressing a firm kiss on her glossy pink mouth.

Somehow they squeezed through the crowd and made it out to the other room.

Everyone swarmed around and Zac escaped to fetch his new wife a drink. He caught Harper watching them with an unreadable expression on her face.

'OK, sweetheart?'

She wrapped her arms around his waist.

'I'm happy. Are you happy?'

'Very.'

'Me, too,' Rebecca whispered over his shoulder. 'Is it all right for me to join in?'

Harper nodded and Zac opened one arm to draw Rebecca into the fold.

'Don't tell anyone but Santa Claus came early and brought us everything we wanted,' Zac fake-whispered and tugged on Rebecca's skirt. 'Lucky he didn't try to stuff you into my stocking or he'd still be struggling this time next year.'

Harper giggled.

'Silly Daddy.'

'We're in complete agreement there,' Rebecca announced.

Two against one. Zac saw the way things were going and couldn't be happier.

We do hope that you have enjoyed reading this large print book.

Did you know that all of our titles are available for purchase?

We publish a wide range of high quality large print books including:
Romances, Mysteries, Classics
General Fiction
Non Fiction and Westerns

Special interest titles available in large print are:
The Little Oxford Dictionary
Music Book, Song Book
Hymn Book, Service Book

Also available from us courtesy of Oxford University Press:
Young Readers' Dictionary
(large print edition)
Young Readers' Thesaurus
(large print edition)

For further information or a free brochure, please contact us at:
Ulverscroft Large Print Books Ltd.,
The Green, Bradgate Road, Anstey,
Leicester, LE7 7FU, England.
Tel: (00 44) **0116 236 4325**
Fax: (00 44) **0116 234 0205**

When troubled army veteran and musician Josh Robertson returns home to Nashville to be the best man at his younger brother Chad's wedding, he's sure that he's going to mess it all up somehow. But when it becomes clear that the wedding might not be going to plan, it's up to him and fellow guest Louise Giles to save the day. Can Josh be the best man his brother needs? And is there somebody else who is beginning to realise that Josh could be her 'best man' too?

FARMER WANTS A WIFE

Sarah Purdue

Skye works in London, with no intention of ever going back to the farming life in which she was raised. Then she travels to meet with Charles, a new client who lives in rural Wales. When she crashes her car in heavy snow, she is rescued by Ren and Gethin. Snowbound, she starts helping on their farm — and growing closer to Gethin. But when Skye's business with Charles threatens her new friends' livelihood, she has a hard decision to make . . .

ONE SUMMER WEEKEND

Juliet Archer

Alicia Marlowe's life as an executive coach is well under control — until she meets her new client, Jack Smith. Jack's reputation precedes him, and Alicia knows immediately that he spells trouble. Not least because he reminds her of someone else — a man who broke her heart and made her resolve never to lower her guard again. As long as she keeps Jack in his place, Alicia thinks she might just make it through unscathed. But Jack has other ideas — including a 'business' trip to the Lake District . . .

FALLING ON ICE

Evelyn Orange

Elsa has recently fulfilled two ambitions — to open her own café, and to learn to ice skate. But her life is turned upside down when she takes part in her first competition and bumps into her teenage sweetheart, Daniel. There's still a spark between them — but is she opening herself to having her heart broken again, especially when it begins to look as if Daniel might have something to do with sinister events at the rink? Can Elsa keep her cool and prevent herself from falling on ice?

COURTING THE COUNTESS

Anne Stenhouse

When Melissa Neville, widowed Countess of Pateley, suffers life-threatening injuries in a fire, no one expects her to survive long. However, despite her disfigurement, would-be suitors have been a constant intrusion, all of them hoping to get their hands on her fortune before she expires. Then one night, in the privacy of her bath, she is abducted without explanation by Colonel Harry Gunn and his steward Zed, who specialise in medicine and seem to want to help her. What is their real motive — and can Melissa hope to love again?